the
last  girl

the
Last Virgin

DAVID BELBIN

Hodder
Children's
Books

a division of Hodder Headline Limited

For Jenny and Penny, a Higher Agency.

1

There were six of them in the queue for the multiplex: Megan, Nina, Parvinder, Bethany, Leah and Zoe. There had been six of them since Zoe's fourteenth birthday party at the beginning of Year Nine. Now it was nearly the end of Year Ten and the girls were closer than ever, except in one respect.

'I wonder which of us will be next,' Zoe said.

'It's not a race,' Nina told her.

'If it was,' Bethany reminded her, 'you'd already be the winner.'

'Most girls don't do it till they're seventeen,' Leah told the others. 'And for boys, it's nineteen. Can you imagine waiting that long?'

'Where'd you hear that?' Zoe asked.

'Radio One.'

'Nineteen is ancient,' Nina declared.

'That's how old my mum was when she got married,' Parvinder said.

'See what I mean?' Nina asked the others. 'Wait until

you're nineteen, you might as well wait until you're married.'

Megan listened without comment. Here they were, all fifteen years old. Two of them had done it and four of them hadn't. So Megan was in the majority. Any day now, though, the odds would change to fifty-fifty. And, after that . . .

'I'll bet I'm last,' Leah said. 'I'm always behind everyone else. I didn't get my period until I was practically thirteen.'

'No, it'll be me,' Zoe said. 'I'm waiting until I'm engaged.'

This caused everybody to stop and stare. Zoe was the most lusted after girl in their year. Boys queued up to ask her out. Most got turned down flat. If she was going to wait until . . . Zoe kept a straight face for the best part of a second. Then she cracked up.

'Guess who asked me to a party next Saturday?' she said when they'd all stopped laughing, some more comfortably than others. 'Iain Foster.'

Megan felt a stab of envy but tried not to show it. She'd harboured hopes of Iain Foster herself. But, naturally, he wanted Zoe. So now it was virtually predetermined. Zoe would be the third to go.

The movie was so forgettable that they picked up the

conversation immediately on the way out.

'Don't you feel different?' Megan asked Bethany, whom she'd known since primary school.

'Not really,' Bethany said. 'It was over so fast, I hardly feel like it counts.'

'Oh, it counts all right,' Nina said. 'Listen. Next time . . .'

The crowd of people leaving the cinema forced Megan to one side. She was excluded from the rest of the conversation. But she was already excluded anyway. Zoe fell into step alongside her.

'I never expected Beth to be second,' she muttered.

'I know what you mean,' Megan said. Flat-chested Bethany was the youngest-looking of the group. Her mum was a vicar and her dad taught RE at their school. Bethany's dad actually taught Ross Simm, the lad Bethany had done it with. Her dad would have a heart attack if he knew what his sweet young daughter had been up to. Ross didn't even use a condom (Nina had had to escort Bethany to the clinic for the morning-after pill and a lecture on STDs).

'Why do you think she did it?' Zoe asked Megan.

'Because she likes Ross a lot?' Megan ventured.

'To get it over with,' Zoe corrected.

'Maybe things got . . . out of control,' Megan suggested.

'Or maybe she wanted to catch up with Nina,' Zoe suggested. 'I do sometimes. You know how she gets that *secret knowledge* smile, that "you'll understand when you've got a boyfriend like Tom" look? It annoys me like hell.'

Leah, Megan and Bethany lived on the same bus route.

'So, which of us do you think will be last?' Leah asked at the back of the bus, when they had it to themselves. That was Leah, never able to let anything go.

Nobody answered. Bethany looked embarrassed.

Megan got off the bus first and made the short walk home. Leah's question both fascinated and irritated her. Since Nina first had sex, halfway through Year Nine, whether to do it or not had dominated endless conversations, every time anyone had a new boyfriend.

Megan wasn't obsessed with sex. How many partners you'd had wasn't the only thing which mattered in life, as her parents pointed out whenever they let her watch 'Sex And The City' with them. Love was.

The only person in the group who didn't go on about sex was Nina. She'd been going out with Tom for a year and had better things to discuss than what they got up to in bed. There was Tom's car, the flat he was going to get, the holiday they were going to go on together in the summer.

Meanwhile Megan, at fifteen, had only had two boyfriends. The first, Steve, was in Year Eleven when she was in Year Nine. They'd been out three or four times (depending on whether you counted the disco where he'd turned up drunk, spent five minutes groping her, then become violently sick) before she'd dumped him. Her next boyfriend was only a year older than her. Megan was ready to fall for Rob, but all he was interested in was sex. When Megan told Rob he'd have to wait, he'd dumped her and gone out with Tracey Cook, who'd given him chlamydia (served him right). That was six months ago.

Meeting boys wasn't easy when you weren't the sort of girl who lied about her age in pubs or let loud lads chat you up in the street. Middleton was aptly named, being in the middle of nowhere. There were no cities within striking distance and only one secondary school. At the comp, Megan's choice was limited to the boys in her year (unthinkable) and those in the one above (the comp had no sixth form). Out of Year Eleven, there were only three boys she really fancied. Rob Hatton had been a disaster. Iain Foster didn't seem to know Megan existed. Which left Jack Green. Megan wasn't sure how much she liked him. But he'd asked her out this morning break.

There's this party at Todd Smith's, Saturday. Would you – you know . . . ?

And she'd said, sort of, because it didn't do to be too enthusiastic, *OK*.

Why hadn't she told the others about Jack, either before or after the movie? Was it because Megan didn't want to tread on Bethany's big moment? Maybe. Was it because, despite the closeness of the group's friendship, Megan had a strong secretive streak? Definitely. But it was also because Nina had already been out with Jack. They'd been an item for three weeks before Nina dumped him for that guy who worked at the CD store who, in turn, dumped Nina when he found out that she was only fourteen. Which didn't matter because shortly afterwards, Nina met Tom. Tom didn't care that Nina was four years younger than him. All he saw was a feisty girl with dark, curly hair and a good figure.

Jack sometimes hung around with Iain Foster. Iain had been out with some of the best-looking girls in Year Eleven. And, according to Year Ten gossip, he'd slept with them all. Meg didn't know how many girlfriends Jack had had since Nina. But if he was anything like Iain, he'd expect her to have sex within a week or two.

And maybe Megan would, too.

* * *

'Good film?' Sarah asked when Megan got in.

'Not very.'

'Lizzie called. She wanted to know if you can baby-sit on Saturday night.'

'Can't. I'm going out.'

'Since when?'

'There's this party I've been asked to.'

'First I've heard of it.'

'This lad at school asked me. Jack, in Year Eleven.'

'I see. Rather short notice.'

That was Sarah, always willing to find fault in a promising situation.

'I guess all the other girls he likes turned him down,' Megan joked.

'Or maybe it took him a while to work up the nerve to ask you.'

'Yeah, maybe.' Hard to see Jack as nervous, but he *had* been a little tongue-tied earlier.

Sarah made the enquiries that parents make when their daughters are invited to parties. Megan knew the questions by rote: whose house was it? Would there be adults there? Was she still carrying a condom in her purse, just in case? None of these questions were asked in quite these words (in fact, for some reason, Sarah seemed half-hearted), so it was easy for Megan to duck the answers. In the end, Sarah knew and Megan knew, what Megan did was down to Megan. There was nothing either of her parents could do to protect her if she didn't choose to protect herself. Or if Megan didn't feel like she needed protecting.

'I know what boys of that age are like,' Sarah said. 'Some of them won't take "no" for an answer.'

'According to Leah,' Megan told her, 'most girls lose their virginity two years before boys do. So maybe you ought to worry about *me* corrupting *him*.'

'It's not about corruption,' Sarah said. 'It's about waiting till you're ready. In my day, good girls didn't sleep with anyone until they were at university.'

'*Good* girls?' Megan mocked. 'Who wants to be a *good girl*?'

They both laughed, but Sarah sounded distinctly uneasy.

2

'I've got something to tell you,' Pat told Megan on Saturday evening. 'Sarah and I need to go to Sydney next week, just for a few nights.'

'What, *both* of you?'

Her parents worked together, as design consultants, but normally it was Pat alone who did the promotional presentations, the travel.

'Yes, there's a big job in the offing. A new university building. They want to give both of us the look-over. It might mean a lot of money.'

'I'll be fine on my own for a couple of nights,' Megan filled in quickly.

'Maybe you would. When you're sixteen and you've finished your exams it might be different. Until then . . .'

'I can probably stay with Zoe, or Leah.'

'No, not for four nights – maybe five – with school the next day. It's not fair on them or their parents. I've asked Joe. He's happy for you to stay with him.'

'Joe! But I haven't stayed at his for years.'

'He *is* your godfather,' Pat reminded her. 'You ought to spend more time with him.'

'I dunno.' Compared to most people, Joe was a pushover. He was her parents' oldest friend and had often baby-sat Megan back when Pat and Sarah were starting up their consultancy. There was a time when Megan could have talked to Joe about anything. Once a week, Megan would go to his house after school while Pat and Sarah did volunteer counselling in town.

All that had begun to change when Megan passed puberty. A little distance crept in on both sides. Megan was too busy to stop by often. And when Joe came to the house, she was seldom there. They hadn't exactly become strangers. They just had some catching up to do.

'I guess it'll be all right,' Megan conceded. 'But Joe's spare room is tiny. It was OK when I was a kid but . . . couldn't he stay here?'

'You know he couldn't.'

Joe was partially disabled and parts of his house were specially adapted. He had stair rails, special handles in the shower and bath, no low cupboards or plugs.

'Anyhow, he keeps his computer in the spare room these days,' Pat told her. 'He's had the basement converted into a guest room. Didn't you know?'

'I'd forgotten.' Megan hadn't been to her godfather's since he'd had the work done.

'So, who's this lad you're going out with tonight?'

'His name's Jack. Jack Green. His dad's giving us a lift to the party.'

'You've not mentioned him before, have you?'

'He's in the year above me.' Megan decided not to mention that Jack used to go out with Nina. Pat didn't like Nina and the feeling was mutual. 'He's nice.'

Megan wanted to close the conversation down but Pat wouldn't let go.

'Are you sleeping with him?' she asked.

'This is a first date!' Megan protested.

Pat frowned. 'I remember what it was like, being fifteen,' she said. 'You don't tell your parents half of what you're up to. And I remember what sixteen-year-old boys are like. Make him wait and he'll respect you more.'

'Or chuck me, like Rob did,' Megan pointed out. 'I think that might be his dad's car.'

As she said this, Sarah called from the front room. They were here. In the hallway, Megan's two mothers, one English, one Australian, said goodbye, then watched warily as their daughter went to join her date.

* * *

Jack got out of the car to meet Megan. He had Mum's CKOne on his newly-shaved chin. He hoped the ads told the truth, that the scent was for women *and* for men. He spat out the mint he'd been sucking to cover up the smell of the cigarette he'd just smoked. None of those posh Year Ten girls smoked, which made them harder to get to. You couldn't casually offer one a fag on the field then ask what they were doing Saturday night. He'd had to plot for a week to get Megan on her own.

Even now, he wasn't sure if he'd done the right thing. You were meant to take out girls you could relax with, have a laugh with, but Megan Rhys-Carter was too good-looking for Jack to totally relax, too clever for him to fall into easy conversation with. Then there were her parents . . .

But Jack didn't have to meet the parents. Megan was at the door before he could ring the bell.

'You look great,' Jack told Meg, who was wearing a black camisole and a red, leather skirt. Her long, curly reddish-brown hair was brushed right back, making her look about twenty, though she was only fifteen.

'You don't look so bad yourself,' Megan said, leaning in towards him as Jack opened the rear door for her. He thought for a moment she was going to kiss him on the cheek. 'Is that CKOne?'

Jack blushed. He didn't want Dad to know he was using Mum's perfume.

'Who's going to be at this thing?' Meg asked. Jack rattled off some names. The only one of her crowd who was going to be there was Zoe Cumberland. But, of course, Megan knew that already.

'Are you friendly with Iain?' Meg asked.

'Sort of. He's more into sport than I am.'

Iain's main sport was horizontal jogging, but Jack didn't mention that.

'Whereas you're into . . .'

'Bands. Computer animation. American Indie comics. Stuff like that.'

'What kind of comics?'

Jack couldn't believe it. Girls were never interested in comics. Never. He had already started kicking himself for mentioning them. Now he couldn't stop.

'Not superheroes or kiddie crap like that. I'm into *Stray Bullets*, *Eight Ball*, *The Preacher*. Lots of different stuff.'

'You ought to meet my godfather,' Megan said. 'He's into all that kind of thing. He draws comics, too. Well, cartoons mostly.'

'Really. What's his name?'

Megan told Jack the name and it meant nothing to him, but the ice was well and truly broken. When Dad dropped them off at the party, he put a thumb up and slipped Jack a tenner for a taxi. 'You make sure you get her home safely, hear?'

Jack agreed. He meant to treat Megan like a lady. However, the moment they walked in, he could tell that it wasn't a party for *ladies*. Everybody seemed to be bouncing off the walls. Nu-metal music was playing and there was already beer on Todd Smith's parents' polished wooden floor. Sacking had been put down to cover the dance area but most of that had either been kicked aside or was being worn – in a variety of ways. Taz Newton, from Jack's tutor group, didn't seem to be wearing anything else. Megan looked a little alarmed. Jack tried to smile reassuringly.

'Let's get a drink.' He took Megan's hand and she followed him into the kitchen, a similar scene of devastation. It wasn't yet nine, but all the booze had gone, so Jack decided against depositing his bottle. He found two clean paper cups, then glanced at Megan, who had gritted teeth.

'Want to try the garden?'

She nodded vigorously.

There were only a handful of people in the garden. Todd Smith had his head in his hands – no need to guess why – and was being comforted by Stacey Cooper. Iain Foster was talking to Zoe, the only girl at the party who was wearing a dress. They were drinking what looked like Coke. Zoe waved at Jack and Megan.

'Want to join them?' Jack asked his date.

'Be rude not to,' Megan mumbled.

Iain didn't look too happy about being interrupted. Zoe, however, was talkative enough for two.

'Isn't it mad in there? What have you got to drink? Want to try some of this? We had to keep it with us because it'd only last two seconds in the fridge, but Pimms is no good if it isn't kept cold . . .'

She produced several cans of Pimms No. 1, which Megan accepted enthusiastically. Jack had one too. It tasted like some kind of fruit soda but the can said it was 25% proof, so he gulped it down, wanting the alcohol to relax him.

While Zoe was chatting away, Megan kept glancing at Iain. Did she fancy him, Jack wondered? That was the last thing he needed. Iain Foster, with his square jaw, sculpted cheekbones and jet black hair, could have whoever he wanted, as Zoe's presence proved. Jack couldn't compete.

'Didn't you used to go out with Nina?' Zoe asked, and Jack felt himself begin to blush. Nina had been his first and, to date, only proper girlfriend.

'That was nearly a year ago,' he managed to say.

It was getting dark and mosquitoes were beginning to gather. Gallantly (he thought), Jack lit a cigarette to keep them away. Megan frowned and stepped back half a metre. Jack could tell that he wouldn't be kissing *her* in a hurry. She and Zoe began talking about summer holidays. Iain turned to Jack.

'We can't take them back in there. What do you reckon? Pub?'

Jack hadn't brought much cash. He didn't want to break into the taxi fare his dad had given him. Also, he was aware that, unlike Iain, he looked his age. A pub might not serve him. Luckily, Zoe came to the rescue.

'We can walk to mine from here. My mum and dad should be out by now. Why don't we go there?'

'Good idea,' Megan said, then hesitated and turned to Jack. 'Unless you want to stay . . .'

'No, no, that's fine.'

'I think we can get out by the side, without going through the house,' Iain said. 'Why don't we?'

Megan took Jack's hand again and they followed the other couple out. As they left the garden, Jack glanced into the living room. Todd had rejoined his party with a bang. He seemed to be doing handstands with Taz and Stacey. The music was louder and more people were arriving every moment. It looked like this was going to be the end of Year Eleven party to end all end of Year Eleven parties. And he was leaving early. Jack hoped that Megan would be worth it.

3

Nine fifteen and Ross still hadn't called. Bethany reviewed the arrangement they'd made in case there was any room for confusion.

Can I see you next week? His exact words.

Saturday? Hers.

Great. His last words. Then he was gone. No *I'll call you*, but she had assumed he would, keeping all day Saturday free, waiting for him to ring, wishing that she'd given him her mobile number so that she wasn't bound to stay home. Now she was sat here, in her best jeans and a pink, sleeveless top which emphasised what little breasts she had. What would Nina say? *He got what he wanted and now he isn't interested.* But Ross wasn't like that. He went to a church school. Dad trusted him, which was why he'd left Ross and Bethany to lock up last Monday night.

Bethany replayed the evening in her head. The disco ended at nine thirty. Dad had joined Mum in the Vicarage (they always liked to watch *News at Ten*).

Neither she nor Ross were in a hurry to say goodnight. One minute Ross was telling Beth how he only helped out at these discos because of her. He looked away, shyly, and, acting on some instinct, Beth squeezed his shoulder. Then they were kissing. The next thing she knew, they were on the carpeted floor behind the snack bar and everything was out of control. *News At Ten* was still on when Bethany locked the back door to the church hall and shot upstairs for a shower. Only the next day, when Nina had taken her to the chemists for the morning-after pill, did it sink in.

'The whole thing finished so quickly,' she told her friend. 'He started and the next thing I knew he'd made his mess.'

'Sounds like my first time,' Nina told her. 'Didn't you discuss a rubber?'

'It was over before I even began to think about that.'

'Next time, make him,' Nina urged.

But it didn't look like there was going to be a next time. Bethany rang Parvinder, the only one of her friends likely to be in on a Saturday night.

'So he didn't call?' Parvinder said.

'No. He didn't call.'

'I'm sorry, kid. Want to come over?'

'I dunno. Maybe I'd better stay here, just in case.'

'Don't you know his number?'

'I don't even know his surname,' Bethany admitted.

'I thought your dad taught him.'

'I can't ask my *dad*.'

'You can find a way to ask him without asking,' Parvinder suggested.

'Not now, I can't. He's already gone to bed. Tomorrow's the biggest day of the week. They always turn in early.'

The conversation continued for a few more minutes, then Beth got off the line. She didn't want it to stay engaged for long in case Ross rang.

Zoe was not a risk-taker. She wouldn't have invited Iain Foster to the house if Megan and Jack weren't coming too. She didn't know him well enough. Mum and Dad would be back from the pub in two hours' time, but a lot could happen in two hours. Now the four of them were in the living room, and it wasn't quite clear how things were going to pan out. The obvious scenario – the one that Iain had already urged on her – was that she and he should go up to her room, leaving Meg and Jack alone. But Zoe had already ruled that out, whispering to Iain that it would be rude.

They're my guests. Talk to them.

Conversation, however, was nearly non-existent. Jack looked pissed off, Megan uncomfortable. Iain, on to his second can of strong lager, was taking the strong, silent thing too far. Zoe had let him choose the music, then snogged him several times, allowing one of his hands to explore her right breast (beneath the dress but above the bra). Was she meant to enjoy being pawed like that? Zoe only found it embarrassing, especially with Meg and Jack in the same room. She had no intention of going any further, not on a first date. She'd yet to go further with any boy, but Iain's reputation went before him. He would be hard to say no to. On the stereo, Alicia Keys sang about falling.

'Can I put on something . . . more rocking?' Jack asked, politely.

'Be my guest,' Zoe said. 'Most of the good CDs are in my room.'

She was about to tell Jack where the room was, then realised that she didn't want him looking round her stuff on his own.

'I'll come with you,' Megan said, hurriedly standing. 'If you don't . . .'

'No, fine,' Zoe said, then watched as Meg and Jack shot out of the room.

'That should be us, going up there,' Iain said, before licking her ear. 'They'll be gone for an hour now.'

'I don't think so,' Zoe told him. 'Jack hasn't even tried to kiss her yet.'

'Turn that light off,' Iain suggested. 'They'll get the message.'

Zoe hesitated. She didn't like the way that Iain was telling her what to do in her own home. But then he kissed her, and the other couple didn't come back. She turned the main light off, keeping an eye on the clock. Then, feeling like this was happening to somebody else, Zoe let Iain undo the buttons at the back of her dress.

Jack and Megan walked down the stairs carefully, bodies not brushing against each other, CD in hand. The door, which Megan had left ajar, was closed. Gently, she opened it. The light was off.

'Oh,' Megan said, closing it again. She turned to Jack. 'Maybe we better go back upstairs.'

'OK.'

She thought he might take her hand, but he didn't. The way Nina talked about Jack a year ago, Meg expected him to be all over her, like Iain was with Zoe. Yet so far he had been a perfect gentleman. Perfect was an exaggeration. He smelt of smoke, swore too much, and kept running out of things to say. So did she, though. In the car, coming over, it seemed like they had a lot in common. Turned out their main similarity was that they went to the same school.

The conversation having run dry, there was only one

thing left to do. Jack let his arm tentatively slip over Megan's shoulder. She leant in towards him. His lips were soft. At first it was the perfect kiss, the sort you read out about in beach romance novels. Then her tongue caressed his and she recoiled.

'What's wrong?' he asked.

'Sorry. You taste of smoke.'

'Oh. I could . . . brush my teeth.'

'It's OK,' Meg said.

They kissed again. This time, she kept her tongue back so that the taste wasn't overwhelming. Their chests were pressed closer together. It felt good. Then, one of his hands found its way on to her right thigh, sliding up towards her bottom. That was going way too fast. Meg pulled away from the kiss.

'What's wrong?' Jack said, then protested uselessly. 'I wasn't . . .'

Meg replied without looking at him. 'I guess I'm not really in the mood. It's weird, being up here like this.'

'I know what you mean,' Jack said. He stood and began looking at the collage of photos above Zoe's bed. 'Is that you? How old were you then?'

Megan looked at the photos, which covered Zoe's life since starting secondary school. She was in a lot of them. The one that Jack was looking at showed her with Zoe and Leah at a Christmas in Year Nine, eighteen months ago. Meg couldn't believe how young she looked.

'I must have been about twelve,' she lied.

'You and Zoe go back a long way, huh?'

'Pretty long.'

They looked at each other. 'Want to go back to the party?' Jack asked.

'Not really,' she said with a dismissive shrug. 'But you do, don't you?'

'There are a lot of my friends there,' Jack said, hesitantly. 'I'd rather be with you, though.'

'No, you wouldn't. Not if I won't . . . you know,' Megan said. 'And I won't. Sorry.'

'Oh.' Jack looked crestfallen, so much so that Megan felt sorry for him and, inexplicably, kissed him again. This time, his mouth didn't taste as smoky. But when the kiss ended, Jack broke away from her, as though acknowledging that he'd used up his compensatory goodnight kiss.

'My dad gave me the money to get you a taxi home,' he said.

'Forget it,' Megan told him. 'I'll give Pat a ring. She'll be here in a few minutes.'

Meg used Zoe's bedside phone. Then she wrote her friend a note. *Hope you had a good time*. 'It's OK,' she told Jack. 'You can go back to the party.'

24

'I'll wait,' he said, sheepishly, 'see you get safely off.'

'There's no need,' Megan assured him. 'Thanks for taking me out.'

'Can we try again soon? A film maybe?'

Distracted, Megan shook her head. She caught herself thinking about what Zoe was getting up to with Iain. Envy: what a cheap, demeaning feeling. She and Jack walked downstairs together, talking quietly so as not to disturb Iain and Zoe. The music seemed to have stopped. Jack stood by the door, looking disappointed, like he didn't want to leave and was grasping for conversation.

'What's it like, having two mums?' he asked.

'Normal,' Meg said. 'I don't know any different.'

'But you must have a dad somewhere, right?'

'I don't think of him as a dad. I think of him as a sperm donor.'

This wasn't true, but it was the quickest way of changing the subject. She didn't want to have this conversation now. 'Thanks for taking me out,' she added.

She kissed Jack on the cheek, making it clear that, this time, that was all he was going to get. Jack made too much noise closing the door. Iain and Zoe were bound to hear. Meg stood in the porch, watching Jack walk away, waiting for Pat to show. Then she became aware of someone standing behind her and turned.

'Zo?'

Her friend had been crying. Black mascara zig-zagged from each eye.

'What happened? Did he . . . hurt you?'

Zoe shook her head. 'No. He left.'

'You and Iain didn't . . . ?'

'My mouth tastes horrible,' Zoe said. 'I need a drink.'

'Iain left?' They went into the kitchen, poured orange juice from a carton.

'He went back to the party,' Zoe said.

Outside, a car hooted. Pat. Megan went to the window, waved.

'Is everything all right?' she asked her friend.

'Fine.' Zoe was cleaning her face.

'You and Iain aren't . . .' Megan hated not finishing sentences, but didn't want to put the question into words, unless she'd misunderstood.

'No, we aren't anything,' Zoe said, with a brief, sarcastic laugh.

Pat sounded the horn again and Zoe seemed to wake up. 'Where's Jack?'

'He went back to the party, too. We didn't really hit it off.'

'I'm sorry. Go on, go. I'm fine. Honest.'

Megan hugged her friend, then left, confused.

'How was it?' Pat asked in the car.

'Not my kind of party,' Megan said. 'Not my kind of bloke.'

The place was a wreck. People were using the outside walls to piss against. Jack could smell vomit. There was no sign of Todd, whose house it was. He looked at his watch. Nearly eleven. That meant there would be another surge in a few minutes, when the pubs threw out. Jack felt worryingly sober. Everyone around him was off their head. He needed a drink. But there was none left. Maybe someone would bring a carry-out from the pub.

Loud garage banged from the living room. There was barely room to move. Jack scanned the dancers for familiar faces. Taz Newton was all over some bloke, not Todd who she'd been dancing with earlier. She looked legless. As the song ended, the bloke pulled Taz towards the hall, up the stairs. Jack realised that the guy dragging her was Iain. Hadn't Zoe been enough for him? Jack wasn't built like Iain. He couldn't go from liking one girl to picking up another. He wondered where he'd gone wrong with Meg, what he could have done differently. Then Tracey Cook came over and asked him for a dance.

'I'm not in the mood,' he said.

'I've got a stash of Aftershock in the garden,' Tracey told him. 'That'll put you in the mood, if nothing else will.'

And she was right. It did. Three drinks later, Jack was very relaxed and halfway between smashed and slaughtered. He'd already told Tracey about his failed date with Meg. The two of them were on a wooden bench at the far end of the garden and somehow Tracey had ended up on his lap. Tracey was a slapper. She'd been around. But what was wrong with that? Plain Tracey, with her micro skirt, boobs busting out of her low-cut top, was beginning to look very good indeed.

'Most Year Ten girls don't know what to do with a decent lad,' Tracey told Jack, laying on the flattery. 'I've always liked you. You're not one of those users.'

'Thanks,' Jack said, as Tracey wriggled, arousing him.

'You're going to be glad you ended up with me,' Tracey said.

They kissed. Her hands began to explore beneath his shirt. Jack realised that the condoms in his wallet might not be wasted after all.

4

The gossip was all over school by morning break. Many Year Ten girls saw Zoe as smug and stand-offish, too attractive for her own good. The fact that Iain had ended the evening with gawky but always-up-for-a-laugh Taz Newton was music to their ears. Zoe affected not to give a damn. The same girls used to call her gay when she started hanging out with Meg. It was Leah, always expert at gathering gossip, who broke the other news to Meg. They were on the top deck of the bus home.

'I hear you knocked back Jack. Want to know who he ended up with?'

'It's none of my business,' Meg said, though she hadn't figured Jack would get off with anyone. Most of the girls at the party were already in couples.

'Tracey Cook. Liam Holmes dumped her earlier and she got off with Jack after he'd had a few drinks.'

'Where'd you hear this?' Meg asked. Drunken gossip got exaggerated. Jack had probably given Tracey a goodnight kiss, that was all.

'Lucy Newton and her boyfriend went to use the bench at the back of the garden,' Leah explained. 'They saw the two of them shagging. Sorry.'

'Nothing to be sorry about,' Meg said, standing up. 'I'm glad he didn't have a totally wasted evening, even if he did end up going with a slag. See you.'

'You've two stops yet,' Leah pointed out.

'I'm staying with Joe,' Meg said. She pressed the stop button then descended the stairs without saying goodbye.

Meg let herself into Joe's house with a key.

'Hey, Joe!' She called from the narrow hallway. 'I'm here.'

'C'mon up.' Joe would be at his computer, or drawing board. Meg didn't like to disturb him, but could hardly go straight down to the basement without saying 'hello'. She dumped her bag in the hall and climbed the stairs, passing framed posters for films from the 70s: *Bad Timing*, *Taxi Driver*, *Harold and Maude*. Pride of place went to a black-and-white one for Joe's favourite band, The Who. It read *Maximum R'n'B!* The house was a two-bedroom semi, built on a hill. Megan poked her head into what used to be the spare bedroom, but was now a workroom, with two computers, a printer, fax and other paraphernalia. Joe was hunched over the newer of the two computer screens, a perspex rectangle with an Apple logo.

'I'll make a brew,' she said.

At least he was out of bed. Her godfather had never been a normal grown-up and was becoming less so as Meg grew older. He was his own boss and frequently shlepped around in his dressing gown all day, working when he felt like it, going back to bed if he was short of ideas and thought a nap might help.

Out of old habit, Megan did a quick whirl around the house, tidying up. Joe took great pleasure in throwing things at rubbish bins, rather than dropping them in. He was a pretty good shot, but that still left a lot of debris on the floor. If it built up too much, Joe was liable to trip over something. Megan collected three Fed-Ex packages, binned several crisp packets, put a week's worth of newspapers in the recycling box, then stacked up several books on the one available bit of space, which was a corner of the dining room table. In the kitchen, she put the kettle on before setting to the washing up. Joe refused to have a dishwasher. Reaching down to load or unload it would be difficult for him. But he hated washing up, too. Megan put a pile of food-encrusted plates in to soak before taking two mugs of tea back upstairs.

Joe was still on the computer. He had a cable modem

permanently connected to the internet. Occasionally, he scanned a cartoon and sent it to the magazine which wanted to use it. Most preferred him to mail the original drawing. All day, Joe surfed the net: reading news groups, talking in chat-rooms, shopping, downloading MP3s, checking out other cartoonists' work on the web. The *New Yorker* had a cool site that flashed up a new cartoon every thirty seconds.

'Pull up a chair, sweetcake,' he said, using a pet name from before primary school. There was a spare chair but pulling it out wasn't easily done. The floor was covered with small piles: letters, comics, trade magazines. Megan compromised by leaning on the chair and looking at what Joe was doing.

'Is that what I think it is?'

'Don't ask.' Joe clicked the little box in the top left hand corner, getting rid of the naked, big-breasted woman standing over a pile of tyres. Then he swivelled round on his chair, a thin man in need of a haircut. 'I draw what they ask me to draw,' he told her, with a shy, apologetic smile. 'Believe me, I'd prefer to be in a position where I could turn work like that down.'

'I believe you,' Meg said. 'Did Sarah drop my stuff off?'

'On their way to the airport, yeah. They put it down in the basement flat.'

'Flat? I thought you'd converted the basement into a spare room.'

'Sort of. But it has its own entrance, so I call it a flat. Want a look?'

'Please.'

Joe activated the answering machine on his computer and, awkwardly, got up from his chair. He was wearing a T-shirt which read: *I'm wearing black until they come up with something darker*. Joe moved his left leg stiffly and Meg offered him her arm. He shook his head. 'Foot's gone to sleep. Give me a moment.'

At one time Pat and Sarah had urged Joe to buy a one-level flat as it would be easier on his bum leg. Joe insisted that the exercise did him good and, as if in defiance, bought this house on a steep hill, overlooking the park. The ground floor was on street level, but the basement backed on to a small garden. Until recently, the only thing Joe kept down there was a washing machine. Then his dad died, and he'd used the inheritance to convert the basement into what Meg was about to see.

As they walked downstairs, Joe told her why he'd had the conversion done. 'I keep these odd hours. So I figured that, when friends come to stay, the last thing I want is them disturbing me at work or having to wait for me to finish in the bathroom. So it has its own shower room and a TV, video too.'

'You'll never have to see me,' Megan joked, as they reached the bottom.

'I was kind of hoping that we could catch up with each other,' Joe told her. 'It's been a while since . . . Here, what do you think?'

Meg looked around. 'I hadn't realised it would be so big.'

'Biggest floor of the house. Lots of people on the street have converted them. Course, there can be a problem with damp . . .'

As Joe rambled on, Megan looked around. The basement had its own sink, kettle, phone, TV, video, wardrobe, double bed and wide windows looking out on to wooden decking. Beyond was the park. Tall trees gave them some privacy from the dog-walkers. Meg's portable stereo was on the bed, already plugged in.

'Fantastic place for a party,' Megan muttered aloud, then realised that Joe had stopped talking. Her godfather laughed.

'Easy on now. You're only here for a few nights.'

'It's great. How many people have you had to stay?'

'You're the first. I mean, I only had it converted back in March. I've spent a few nights down here. It was a nice change but—'

'I like the carpet,' Megan interrupted, for there was nothing to dislike about the beige carpet. 'But the walls are a little bare. Have you thought about some posters or . . .'

'I didn't want to impose my taste on it,' Joe said. 'I might want to rent the flat out sometime, when I haven't got much money coming in.'

There'd been times, over the years, when Joe had been on his uppers, living on baked beans and toast. He'd visit Megan's home for free meals every week. Occasional poverty was one of the drawbacks of the life he chose, Joe used to explain. It was a choice for an artist: prostitution or poverty.

Back then, this had confused her, but now she knew what he'd meant by prostitution: drawing pictures of big-breasted naked women to sell remoulded tyres.

'How's school?' Joe asked, as Megan began to unpack her stuff.

'Quiet. Year Eleven are on study leave as of today.'

'So you're the top dogs now?'

'That doesn't mean much,' Megan told him. 'I mean, school – it's just something to get through, isn't it? Kind of like waiting for real life to begin.'

'You shouldn't think that way,' Joe said. 'People can spend their whole life waiting for the real thing to begin.'

Megan gave a wry laugh. She liked having pseudo-philosophical chats with Joe. It had been a while.

'So what do you want to eat tonight?' Joe asked.

'Can we send out for pizza?'

'I'll get the menu.'

Ross ate his tea while watching *The Simpsons*. Sausages, a fried egg, oven chips and baked beans on the side, normally a firm favourite. Today, however, his appetite was off. Ross played with his second sausage. Bart's encounters with Krusty the Clown seemed timeworn and pathetic.

'Are you going to the church disco tomorrow night?' his sister asked, acting as though she could read his mind.

Ross mumbled something deliberately incomprehensible. Then he stuffed his face with the last food on the plate and went upstairs. He didn't want Mum knowing he'd been going to the disco at St Ulrich's because of his crush on the vicar's daughter. Last Tuesday, when he'd stayed behind to help clear up, the most he'd hoped for was a chat with Bethany. Instead, things had progressed beyond his wildest dreams. He still shivered to think about it.

How could he face Bethany again? She was probably as embarrassed by what had happened as he was. He couldn't remember much about afterwards. He'd tried to ask if it was OK for him to come back the following week, to see her again. Instead, she'd said 'Saturday'. He'd said 'great', assuming that there was something on at the church then. But there wasn't. And he couldn't call her up, not when her dad was his RE teacher and her mum was his minister. Even worse was the idea of showing up at the vicarage and asking for her. He wasn't even sure if he could face her in any circumstances. Ross didn't think that what he and Bethany had done was wrong, not exactly. But a lot of people would.

Earlier that evening, while they were putting away chairs, he'd asked why she didn't go to the same school as him.

'Go to the school where my dad works? No thanks. And I get enough religion at home. Where I go, a few of my friends know what my mum and dad do, but they don't make a big deal of it. That's my parents' life, not mine.'

'You still come to the church disco.'

'Only since you started coming.'

'Oh.' That was the moment when he realised that she liked him and maybe, just maybe, something would happen. But why did it have to happen so quickly? The kiss had taken him by surprise. As for the rest . . . it wasn't like he hadn't gone along with it, but Bethany definitely made all the running. She must be experienced. He couldn't imagine the girls at his school being so . . . forward. And if she was experienced, what happened was bound to have badly disappointed her. Never mind going to the disco tomorrow, Ross doubted that he'd ever work up the nerve to speak to Bethany again.

5

'I don't understand why you blew off a perfectly good guy like Jack,' Leah said, stretching out on the double bed beside Megan. She'd come back to the flat after school so that they could work on their Media Studies project.

'We didn't really click,' Megan explained.

'You fancy him, don't you?'

'Yes, but . . .' Meg changed the subject. 'Beth was quiet on the bus today.'

'She's desperate to see if Superboy turns up at the disco tonight,' lanky Leah said, kicking off her shoes. 'It doesn't quite fit, does it? Bethany and the Casanova of the Christian disco circuit.'

'Beth only started helping out because she saw Ross there and fancied him.'

'How come he offered to help too?' Leah asked, unconvinced.

'He's new in town. Beth's dad teaches him. Maybe he suggested it.'

There was a knock on the flat's outer door, which Meg had left open. Joe, wearing a dirty T-shirt and sweat pants, came in before Megan could respond.

'Just made some coffee. Thought you might like—' Seeing a strange girl splayed out on the bed, he blushed. 'Sorry. Didn't know you had company.'

'It's fine,' Megan said, as Leah sat up and straightened her skirt. 'This is Leah. We're working on a project. Is there enough coffee for three?'

'I'll put a bit more on. Two minutes.'

'What a mess!' Leah said, when Joe was gone. 'You need to give him a complete makeover.'

'Joe works from home all day,' Megan told her. 'He's never been bothered about his appearance.'

'How does he get a girlfriend?'

'He doesn't, at least not very often.'

'But he's not . . . like Pat and Sarah?'

'Dunno,' Megan said, shrugging. 'I've never actually asked him.'

'This is such a great flat,' Leah said, rapidly changing the subject. 'If Joe's your *god*father, maybe you could stay here all the time?'

'There's no *if*,' Megan said.

'I wasn't being funny,' Leah protested. 'I just meant, are you sure Joe isn't . . . ? No, forget I said anything. Shall we start on this?'

They began laying out pages. Megan knew what question Leah had been about to ask, and was glad to let it slide. Most of her friends maintained a tactful silence about Meg's paternity. They let Meg tell them as much as she wanted to tell. From the time Meg started school, she'd learnt there were people you mustn't tell. Even before she understood what sex was, on the rare times when she had friends stay for sleepovers, Meg used to ask Pat and Sarah to play down their relationship.

Inevitably, though, people at primary school found out. Some kids blanked her, or worse. It had taken until the second year of secondary school for Meg to find friends who judged her by who she was, not what her parents were. And now it looked like she'd have to deal with the whole issue all over again. Jack's well-meaning *What's it like, having two mums*? was bound to keep coming up with the boys she dated. Meg wished the whole thing would go away.

What *was* it like, having two mums? As she'd told Jack, Meg didn't know any different. Pat and Sarah got on well with each other, and were easy to be around. They answered Meg's questions about sex and sexuality whenever they came up. But there was one thing they couldn't tell her about. Unlike some of their lesbian friends, neither Pat nor Sarah had ever slept with a man. For them, contraception was a theoretical discussion, not a practical one. Sure, they could offer advice about teenage boys and how they behaved. But it was very limited.

'Do you ever talk with your dad about sex?' Meg asked Leah.

'You must be joking,' Leah said.

'But does he, y'know, warn you about what lads are like?'

'Like they're only interested in one thing? Everybody knows that anyway. Dad wouldn't let me work at his place this summer because he says he can't trust his staff around me. I think that was meant to be flattering, but I should be so lucky . . .'

Meg took the top off the spray mount and pointed at two photos of Brad Pitt that they were considering for the cover of their project magazine.

'OK, I want complete honesty. Which do you fancy the most?'

'I think we should use the one where he's with Jennifer Aniston.'

'It's meant to be a magazine aimed at girls,' Meg pointed out.

'*So*? Do you only want to attract straight girls?'

Meg laughed and admitted that her friend had a point.

* * *

Tom and Nina had been bowling. It was a school night, so he dropped her off at ten. Nina rang Bethany on her mobile as soon as she was in her room.

Nina so wanted Bethany's thing with Ross to work out. She and Bethany had been best friends since infant school. They'd done everything together. Other girls fell out, grew apart, graduated to those stuck-up cliques, all except her and Bethany. Until the end of Year Eight, when Nina started going out with boys but Bethany never got asked. That was when the problems started.

At first, it was OK. Nina was better developed, more outgoing. It was inevitable that she would begin dating first. As Year Nine began and they had lessons in option groups instead of forms, Bethany got pally with a new group of girls, the ones who'd adopted Meg, who Nina had never got along with. Nina was hacked off at first: the vicar's daughter was hanging out with all these clever, middle class kids who liked to call her Beth. But the new gang were welcoming enough. And they were different. Nina had never had an Asian friend before. She'd even learnt to like Meg, with the two lesbian mothers. They'd eat her alive on Nina's council estate, but *live and let live* as her mum said.

And the gang took the heat off the things that Nina could no longer share with Bethany. By the time

Nina started seeing Tom, Bethany still hadn't had a boyfriend. Nina could no longer tell her everything. It would feel like she was rubbing it in. These days, inevitably, Tom was Nina's best friend. He'd become part of the family. Mum liked him. She knew what they got up to and – now that Nina was sixteen – tolerated it, even reminding Nina to keep her prescription of the pill up-to-date.

It had never occurred to Nina that Bethany would be next. Megan maybe. She was attractive and kind of free-thinking. Or Leah, definitely. She was gagging for it, the minute she met someone she really liked. Perhaps Zoe, who could have anyone, but claimed to be waiting for Mr Right. It wouldn't surprise Nina if Zoe had already done it, but kept it a secret from the others – she had a secretive streak. Everyone but Parvinder seemed likely to do it before Bethany. Yet then, out of the blue, along came Ross. He went to another school. Nobody even knew what he looked like. Bethany mentioned him once in passing. The following week she was seducing him at the back of the church hall.

Bethany answered her mobile on the second ring. 'Hi, Neen.'

'What happened?'

'Nothing happened. He didn't show up.'

'You didn't hear from him?'

'He's had a week. You always say, if a bloke hasn't called after a week . . .'

'I know . . .' Nina's rules were backfiring on her. 'Maybe he's sick.'

'He got the thing he wanted and he's gone. Maybe what turned him on was seducing his teacher's daughter, or the vicar's daughter. I don't know.'

'That's twisted,' Nina said, though it made a kind of sense.

'Maybe if I hadn't been so eager he'd still—'

Bethany was crying, Nina could tell. She said comforting things, but they didn't help much. Then they cursed Ross whatever-his-name-was, which helped a little. By the time they got off the phone it was nearly eleven. Nina didn't know how she'd explain the length of the call when the bill came next month.

6

Pat and Sarah were asleep when Meg got back from school on Friday, their body clocks thrown by the time difference. A note was on the table: *Wake us when you get in*. Megan took them tea in bed.

Pat had thrown the covers off and was sprawled sideways. Megan used to see Pat and Sarah naked all the time when she was younger, but now it was unusual. Pat was nuzzled against Sarah's side. When she moved her head, a roll of soft flesh moved with her. Sarah had put on weight of late. Meg wondered whether *her* body would widen that way when she was older.

'Tea,' she said softly, pushing the door fully open. Neither mum responded. Meg put down the tea-tray as loudly as she could, clanging mug against mug.

'Welcome home,' she announced. Pat stirred first. Sarah rubbed her eyes.

'How was your trip?' Meg asked, after the ritual cuddle.

'Good,' Sarah said, pulling on a white T-shirt. 'I think they want us.'

'To do what?' Meg asked.

'Later,' Pat replied, yawning. 'How did you get on with Joe?'

'Fine,' Meg said. 'The basement flat's really cool.'

'We thought you'd like it,' Sarah said, adding extra sweetener to her tea. 'I hope you spent some time with him, too.'

'Actually, we got on really well,' Meg said. Which was true. She'd hung out with Joe a lot, played on his computer, eaten pizza and curry. Last night they'd shared a bottle of wine and watched *Klute* on DVD. 'It was nice to catch up.'

Pat and Sarah exchanged a glance which meant something, Meg knew better than to ask what. They began telling Meg about the things they'd done while they were away – meals, an old friend they'd had lunch with, the movies they'd shown on the plane, everything but the job they'd flown over to pitch for. Sarah was Australian. Megan had dual nationality, but hadn't been to Australia since she was twelve. Dual nationality, her parents had explained, meant that if Meg ever wanted to live in Australia, she could.

It wasn't until the evening that Pat and Sarah dropped the bombshell.

'They offered us the job,' Pat told her.

'Great,' Megan said.

'There's one drawback, though,' Sarah joined in.

'What?'

'They want us to start soon – both of us.'

'Why *both*? I mean, there's fax, and e-mail . . . ?' Meg was confused.

'They want us both,' Sarah said. 'We explained about you. They offered to pay for your schooling at a good place. We said it wasn't as simple as that.'

'I can't change school halfway through GCSEs! I can't leave my friends!'

'We know that,' Pat said, in her most mollifying voice. 'And we wouldn't dream of asking you to.'

Megan blinked. What they *would* dream of was starting to slowly sink in.

'Why don't we talk about this tomorrow when we've had a chance to—' Pat started.

'We'll both be jetlagged tomorrow,' Sarah interrupted. 'Meg, here's the deal. The three of us go over in August, once we've fulfilled our commitments here. Have a great holiday. Then you stay with Joe until we return.'

'How long will that be?' Meg heard herself ask, her head reeling.

'Best bet, three months,' Sarah suggested, unconvincingly.

'Christmas at the very latest,' Pat said.

'That's a whole term!' Meg protested.

'You could come and stay at half-term,' Sarah said. 'Look, I'm sorry we're springing it on you like this, sweetheart, but it's your decision. We wouldn't leave you here with Joe unless you're absolutely happy about it. We'll miss you terribly, only it's an awful lot of money.'

'How much?' Meg asked, bluntly.

They told her. It *was* an awful lot of money. Most parents, Meg figured, wouldn't give their only child a choice in a matter like this. Love it or shove it.

'Will you sleep on it?' Pat asked. She had the grace to seem embarrassed by the emotional blackmail stunt that the two of them were pulling.

'Have you asked Joe?' Meg asked. 'How do you think *he'll* feel about me living with him for three months?'

'Joe offered in the first place,' Sarah said.

'He *knew* about this?'

'We mentioned that it was a possibility,' Pat replied. 'He said he'd be happy for you to use the flat whenever you wanted, that he'd like to be a bigger part of your life. Which is as it should be, I guess. After all, he is your father.'

Sarah turned to Pat and gave her a stern look. A kind of stunned silence descended on the room. The *f* word had never been used like that before, not without *god* or *biological* in front. It felt wrong. Megan stood up, her dinner unfinished.

'I'm going to my room,' she told them. 'I'll sleep on it, like you said.'

Why had Pat suddenly used the *f* word? Meg worried, for the first time in ages, that her parents might be about to split up. Sarah was her biological mother, but Meg regarded both of her parents as equal, in every sense. They had chosen to have her together, which was what counted. Joe was their friend, their sperm donor. But Joe wasn't on the birth certificate. Legally, he had no rights as a father. Morally, he had no obligations. Yet he had wanted to be involved in Meg's life, had baby-sat from when she was old enough to be left with him, had been, in fact, the ideal godfather. Not a *father*. She'd never needed one of those.

Pat and Sarah being away was bound to mess up her school work. Meg was determined, disciplined, but she'd miss them terribly. On the other hand, there *was* the prospect of a long holiday in Australia and her own flat for three or four months. Meg didn't know what to say. That was why you slept on something – so that your true feelings would make themselves known to you when you'd stopped consciously thinking about them. Only trouble was, Meg couldn't get to sleep.

Jack was worried that he'd blown it. English Lit was one of his best subjects. He'd done OK on Shakespeare and the novel, but the Carol Ann Duffy question had thrown him. Iain fell into step beside him as they left the exam hall.

'Did you do the question on *We Remember Your Childhood Well*?' Jack asked him.

'No, I wrote about that really sarky one, *Translating The English*. Easy.'

Jack had the impression that, for Iain, everything was easy.

'You still seeing Megan?' Iain asked.

Jack hesitated. No-one liked to tell another bloke he'd been given the bum's rush. Though, come to think of it, Zoe had kicked Iain into touch just as decisively as Meg had dumped him.

'Not really. Why?'

'I was thinking of asking her out.'

'You know she's Zoe's best mate,' Jack put in, quickly, ignoring the stab of jealousy he felt at the thought of Meg going out with Iain.

'So? She's not frigid like Zoe, is she?' Iain asked, rhetorically.

'All I meant . . .' Jack began, then decided not to explain himself. Whatever went down that night between Zoe and Iain, Zoe was bound to have told Meg. So she'd know what he was like. 'Gotta go,' Jack said. 'I need a word with Tracey.'

Tracey Cook was leaving the same exam, alone. Jack hadn't spoken to her since the night of Todd's party. Tracey had her head down because it was raining. She was nearly seventeen but her baggy, old, green kagoul made her look much younger. It was hard for Jack to get her attention without hurrying over and tapping her on the shoulder. He resorted to calling out when he got near enough.

'Hey, Trace!'

Tracey turned round. 'What do you want?' she asked, bluntly.

'Can I walk you home?' he said, realising as he spoke that he had no idea where she lived.

'I get the bus,' Tracey replied.

'Can I walk with you to the bus stop then?'

'I guess.' Tracey looked at him suspiciously.

Now that he had her to himself, Jack didn't know what else to say. He considered saying how good it'd been the other night, but that had too much potential to come out wrong. The moment they were out of the school grounds, Tracey got out a packet of

Marlboro Lights and offered him one.

'Beat me to it.' He took a fag and fumbled for his lighter.

'Spit it out, then,' she said, when he'd lit her up.

'I thought you might like to go out sometime?' he said, tentatively.

'You've left it a while, haven't you? Waiting to see if that Megan would change her mind?'

'That wasn't . . .' Jack could feel himself blushing. He knew Tracey's reputation, but he'd never really believed it. At school, any girl who had more than one boyfriend over the course of a year was immediately deemed to be a slag. Didn't mean she *was* one. Lads lied about sex. OK, Tracey was drunk the Saturday before last, but Jack wasn't the only bloke on his own. He was the one she'd picked. They hadn't gone all the way. But they'd come as close as you could on a bench, with people around. That must mean that there was something between them.

Tracey grinned, enjoying the sight of Jack dangling. 'Tell me something,' she said. 'Why didn't you ask me out before?'

It was true, Jack would never have asked her out if school wasn't over. Too many people would take the piss. 'I didn't realise you were interested until—'

'We were both off our heads. It doesn't count.'

'Oh.' Jack didn't know what to say next. The long summer stretched ahead of him. He had no other prospective girlfriend. Tracey, he'd hoped, would show him the ropes. But the way things were going, he'd still be a virgin at seventeen.

'I've started seeing this bloke I met at the gym,' Tracey said, matter of factly. 'He's got a good job, says he's gonna take me loads of places.'

'Oh.' Jack felt gutted. After that night, he'd kind of assumed that Tracey was his for the asking.

They were at the bus stop. A bus was coming. Tracey, to his surprise, kissed him on the cheek. 'It was nice, but it's not going to happen again. OK?'

'OK.'

Jack stood and watched as the bus pulled away. He felt about two inches tall. The first girl he'd gone out with, Nina, had left him for an older bloke after only three weeks. Now, Tracey – who was hardly a prize catch – was doing the same thing. Before he could lapse further into self-pity, somebody slapped him on the back. Jack turned round. Iain, who had obviously been watching, gave him a reptilian grin.

'I dunno, Jack. First Meg gives you your marching orders and now you can't get a date with the school ho. Tell you what, why don't you hang around until the end of school? Some of those Year Nine girls are pretty fully-developed by now. I'm sure they'd welcome a man of your experience.'

Jack felt like punching him, but Iain was bigger and harder than he was and they were supposed to be mates. So he restricted himself to saying:

'Meg wouldn't be seen dead going out with you. She's got more class.'

'You don't know you're born,' Iain said, raising his hands and playfully pinching both of Jack's cheeks. 'She's gagging for it.'

Jack prayed that he was wrong.

7

'When are you going?' Leah asked.

'A day before term ends.'

'For the whole summer?'

'Not quite.'

'What am I gonna do without you?' Leah let out a plaintive little sigh.

'Everyone goes away in the summer anyhow.'

'You don't, not normally,' Leah pointed out. 'And it's not just you. Parvinder's going to Pakistan. Zoe's going to be in Tuscany for a month. Nina's got a job, then her mum's letting her go off to the Lake District with Tom. Whereas I've got a week with the whole family in Cornwall. And when I come back, there's only Beth to hang out with.'

'Sorry. You and Bethany can have a good time, though, can't you?'

'Maybe,' Leah moaned. 'But Beth can be so wet sometimes. And last time I spoke to her, she was still moping about that Ross.'

'The mysterious Ross who nobody's ever seen,' Megan said. 'Maybe he's worth moping over.'

Pat called from downstairs. 'Meg! Phone.'

Meg didn't get many calls on the land line. Most of her friends used the mobile, because it gave them more privacy. Which meant this was somebody who didn't know her mobile number. She ran downstairs and answered breathlessly.

'Meg, hi. It's Iain Foster.'

'Oh. Hi.'

'I wondered whether you'd like to see a film with me on Saturday night?'

'Um . . .' Meg didn't know what to say. 'In the middle of your exams?'

'My exams finish next week. There're only a couple left. It's no sweat.'

'Right.' She began to think rapidly. 'Did you say Saturday night?'

'If you're not doing anything else.'

Megan didn't know how to react. A month ago, if Iain had asked her out, she'd have said yes straight away, cancelled anything which needed to be cancelled. But that was before whatever happened with Zoe and, anyway, *shit* . . .

'I can't do Saturday. It's my godfather's birthday. Pat and Sarah are doing a big dinner . . .'

'Your *god*father?'

'That's right. Another time?'

'I'm going to Ibiza with some mates for ten days on Thursday. I'll call you when I get back. Can I have your mobile number?'

'Sure.' Meg gave it to him. 'But by the time you get back, I'll be in Australia, I'm afraid. So you won't see me until the end of August.'

'The end of August? That's a long time to be away. You must like it there.'

'I *am* half-Australian,' Meg said. 'Did you know that?'

'No,' Iain said. 'I didn't. I guess there are a lot of things I don't know about you. But I'd like to find them all out.'

'I'm flattered,' Meg told him. 'I'll tell you what, if you're still interested in six weeks' time, call me.'

'I'll do that,' Iain said. 'Have a good holiday.'

'You too. And good luck with your exams.'

Back in her room, Meg recounted the whole conversation word for word.

'You've been interested in him since Year Nine,' Leah teased.

'Year Eight,' Meg confessed.

'And now he's asked you out. I guess it's true: good things *do* come to those who wait.'

'Maybe.' Megan sat on the floor and hunched her knees into her chest.

'What's wrong? Is it Zoe?'

'Of course it's Zoe,' Meg replied. 'She's never really said what happened that night with Iain.'

'So ask her.'

'It's not that simple. Zoe keeps everything about boys close to her chest. I mean, suppose she has feelings for Iain? She might think I'm betraying her.'

'Only one way to find out,' Leah said, and Meg knew she was right.

Zoe and Parvinder played tennis at the public courts on the far side of town. They won a set each, then waited for Parvinder's mum to pick them up. Zoe liked Parvinder. She was the only one of the gang who could give her a competitive game. But Zoe also liked to keep her distance. She didn't feel a need to spill every secret thought, not even to a close friend. It wasn't the way she was made.

Others in their gang seemed to wear their hearts on their sleeves. Secrets were taboo. Zoe tried to give the impression that she was opening up as much as they were. Most people liked to talk about themselves so much, they didn't notice when Zoe held back. Parvinder, however, hardly ever talked about herself.

What she *did* do was ask questions, then really listen to the answers.

'How do you feel about Megan going out with Iain?' Parvinder asked, as they waited on the street outside the courts.

'It's her funeral,' Zoe muttered. Earlier in the week, when Megan told her about Iain's phone call, Zoe had said she was fine with it. Meg had always had a bit of a thing for Iain. She needed to find out for herself what he was like.

'He *is* handsome,' Parvinder pointed out, as though Zoe needed telling. 'If we were in the USA, you two would be voted king and queen of the Prom.'

'Then thank God we're not.'

'I didn't think you believed in God,' Parvinder said.

'No, I don't, but I hate the whole way our culture is based on physical beauty. Because I look the way I do, every guy I meet over sixteen wants to nail me. Even a couple of my dad's friends have made suggestive remarks. Can you imagine what that's like? It makes my flesh crawl. As for Iain, looking the way he does, everyone assumes he's a great guy. And *he* assumes all he has to do is offer himself and any girl will drop her knickers for him.'

'I guess that's been his experience,' Parvinder replied calmly. 'So he tried to have it off with you on a first date. It doesn't necessarily make him a bad guy.'

'And what about the fact that he wouldn't take no for an answer?'

Parvinder looked concerned. 'He didn't do anything out of order?'

'It felt out of order to me,' Zoe told her. 'He's no gentleman.'

'You're looking for a *gentleman*?' Parvinder asked.

'Aren't you?'

'My situation's different from yours.'

Zoe used the opportunity to turn the conversation back to familiar territory. 'By which you mean that you'll have an arranged marriage.'

'That's right,' Parvinder said.

'And you're happy about that?'

Her friend shrugged. 'I wouldn't be happy if Mum and Dad married me to some distant relative with no English. But they won't. They'll choose somebody from here, a guy I'll get on with.'

'How can you be sure?' Zoe asked. 'There's more to a relationship than just *getting on* with someone.'

'I know, and, whoever it is, we'll get to see each other before our parents sort things out, make sure that we like the look of each other.'

Zoe wasn't convinced. 'If my parents worked that way, you know who I'd end up with? Iain Foster.'

Parvinder took this seriously. 'If you were a Sikh, the Iain Foster you married wouldn't have had sex with half a dozen girls in Year Eleven. He wouldn't have learnt to treat women the way he does.'

'He'd still be the same guy,' Zoe said. 'And I still wouldn't want to go to bed with him. But let's go back to talking about you. When will you get married?'

'In a couple of years, probably.'

'You won't go to university?'

'Maybe after marrying. Mum and Dad don't want me to have too much freedom. I might be tempted to do things I'd regret later, that's what they say.'

'And you go along with that?'

'Yeah. You have to respect your parents.'

'You'd do really well at university,' Zoe said, as Parvinder's family car pulled up. 'I guess it's time to talk about something else.'

'No, it's OK. We can talk about anything in front of Mum. Really.'

In the car, Mrs Kaur wanted to know all the things Zoe was up to. There was no room to continue the previous conversation.

'I expect you have a big, handsome boyfriend,' Parvinder's mum said, as they pulled up outside her drive.

'Not at the moment,' Zoe told her. 'In fact,

Parvinder's nearly convinced me that I'd be better off if I settled for an arranged marriage, like her.'

Mrs Kaur turned to Zoe, who was in the back seat.

'It's not something you *settle* for, Zoe. It's an informed choice. Instead of being guided by passion, which fades rapidly, you're guided by the reason of people you love and trust.'

'When you put it like that,' Zoe said, getting out of the car, 'it sounds even more attractive. Thanks for the lift. See you Monday, 'Vinder.'

The birthday was Joe's thirty-seventh. Megan hadn't thought much about his age before. Today she did the maths. Take off her fifteen and three quarter years, add nine months of pregnancy, and Joe was twenty-one when she was conceived.

The evening was more of a dinner party than a knees-up. There were eight of them around the pine table in the kitchen. Joe was better dressed than usual, wearing his new, orange, linen shirt (a present from Pat and Sarah) and, in honour of the hot weather, baggy shorts. He'd had a haircut and wore Converse trainers with no socks. He looked presentable, but he didn't look like anybody's dad.

As she sipped wine, Megan thought about the fathers she knew: Zoe's was a banker, balding, with expensive suits and a much younger second wife (Zoe's mum). Bethany's was an RE teacher, and looked like one. Parvinder's dad was handsome and young, not much older than Joe, but he acted like a grown-up, whereas Joe didn't. Leah's dad, admittedly, was an old hippie, with the emphasis on *old*. He wore a ponytail. That was OK, Leah said, because he was a chef. Megan had never met Nina's dad. Neither, according to Nina, had she.

In the dad stakes, Joe would have been enviable when Megan was younger. He had an interesting job and was young enough to have fun with. But now Joe acted *too* young. Meg didn't want her friends to suddenly find out that they were related, because that would lead back to all the stuff that she used to get teased about all the time, especially in her first two years at secondary school. Maybe they ought to have it out tonight, before this thing became a done deal. She would live with Joe for three or four months, but she wasn't going to become his *daughter*.

Sarah came in with a birthday cake. They sang the song. Joe blew out the candles. Everybody kissed him. Joe's friend Eddie, a thirtyish website designer, slapped him on the back and proposed that they crack open the bottle of champagne he'd brought. Meg was last to get a glass, so only ended up with an inch of bubbly. As they toasted her godfather, Meg felt sad. Joe looked lonely. Apart from him and Meg, the guests were in couples. She'd hate it if she were still single at his age.

They moved into the front room and Eddie put on a mix CD he'd made. After a while, everyone danced – except Joe, whose duff leg made dancing impossible. Meg lasted a while but didn't like the music. She joined Joe.

'Having a nice time?'

Joe put an arm around her shoulder. 'All the people I'm closest to are here.'

'Great,' Meg said. She was glad that he was enjoying himself. Unable to think of anything further to say, she leant her head against his. She felt sad that Joe was happy with so little. She was also anxious about how they'd get on, living together for a whole term.

The party dragged. Just as the others were starting to drift back into the other room, Eddie insisted on dancing with Megan. Eddie was a very bad dancer. How, Megan wondered, as Eddie grinned gormlessly and swirled her round, had she convinced herself to turn down a date with Iain Foster for this?

8

Jack had been on holiday for five weeks now, and was making the most of it. Staying in bed until midday was luxury. Watching videos all afternoon was a good crack, too. Iain and a bunch of his mates were in Ibiza, which made Jack envious. The British summer only tended to last two weeks. Today, though, the good weather had arrived. Why waste it?

Jack decided to walk into town. He was wearing his lightest T-shirt, yet soon built up a sweat. He stopped in the CD shop and browsed for a while. Then he realised that, if he was going to spend time in the garden, working on his tan, he needed something to read. He gave the town's small bookshop a miss. Instead he went to the library, an open plan, sixties building with a staircase in the middle and a balcony which went all the way round the first floor, with its study desks and reference books.

She was standing by the Adult fiction, reading the back cover of a novel by Chuck Palahniuk. Who was she? Jack had lived in this town all his life and he'd never seen her before. Tall and stunning, she looked like a sixth former, even a university student. Out of Jack's league, but his curiosity was roused. Who *was* she?

She'd be new in town because she'd come here with a job, Jack decided. But what job? The girl was dressed too casually to work in a bank or estate agents, the main white collar shops on the high street. The other places: bakers, dry cleaner, cafe, all required a uniform. Anyway, it was three in the afternoon. If she had a job, she ought to be at work. Jack took a closer look at the girl. She had long, fair hair, a slightly snub nose, intelligent eyes and an athlete's legs. She was wearing a crop top and he couldn't stop himself eyeing her breasts, which were a little larger than Nina's, the only naked breasts Jack had seen so far. If somebody had lined this girl up alongside every girl Jack fancied at his previous school, Jack would have chosen this one, no contest. He *had* to work out a way of speaking to her.

But libraries weren't places where you picked people up. They were the opposite of clubs or parties. There was an unspoken pact amongst the users that nobody spoke to anybody else, that you were there to study, sleep or read. Raise your voice, and a library assistant was entitled to give a cartoon *sssssshhhh*! No. He mustn't give up. This was the long summer holidays and the girl was probably killing time, just as Jack was. Sometimes you had to risk humiliation. All right, she might be older than him, she might have a boyfriend, she might laugh in his face, but there were four more weeks stretching out ahead of Jack, four long weeks with most of his mates away and no girlfriend in sight.

As he walked towards her, she glanced at him and Jack nearly changed direction. But she kind of smiled before looking back at the book and tucking it under her arm. He was right in front of her now and she was ready to move on. It was now or never. He pointed at the copy of *Fight Club* that she was holding.

'I really liked the film they made of that book. Is he any good? The writer, I mean – I don't suppose you've read the novel yet.' This was already going badly.

'No,' she said. 'No, I haven't.' Her accent wasn't from round here. He couldn't place it. 'He's on the "further reading" list of this course I'm about to start. I thought I might give him a try.'

'What course would that be?' Jack asked. 'University?'

'No.' She smiled, as if flattered. 'Sixth form. The college down the road.'

'Oh,' Jack said. 'I'm going there, too. Presuming I get the grades, that is.'

'Same here.'

She wasn't moving away. He could continue the conversation. Jack hoped he wouldn't run dry, the way he did when he was around Meg.

'I haven't seen you in town before,' he told her. 'Lived here long?'

She shook her head. 'My family moved here a few months ago for my dad's job, but I stayed behind, living at a friend's. Didn't want to mess up my exams by moving schools. I've only been here a fortnight. It seems OK.'

'The place is a bit dead in the summer,' Jack told her. 'Look, I've got *Fight Club* on DVD. It's wide-screen, lots of extra scenes and stuff. Perhaps you'd like to come round and watch it sometime.'

Her eyes twinkled and he knew he was in.

'Sure,' she said. 'Why not?'

'My name's Jack Green, by the way.'

'I'm Harper, Harper Simm.'

'Are you doing anything tonight?'

Some people still thought that it was all right for a boy to call a girl and ask her out but not the other way round, not even in this, the twenty-first century. If you'd got good mates, you could get around the problem by having them ask him to ask you. But most of Leah's mates were away and, anyhow, the only person she could think of who might be decent company and who still seemed to be around town was Jack Green, who had already been out with two of her closest friends. And, nice as Jack was, Leah didn't particularly fancy him. There weren't many boys who Leah really, honestly, fancied. Did that make her choosy or just weird?

Leah wished Zoe and Meg weren't away. They were the two people she was closest to. Zoe was fantastic, but not always easy company. Meg was the most fun. Only Nina and Beth were around, and even Beth had a boyfriend now, though nobody seemed to have met him. There were no parties, no places to hang out that she wasn't either too young or too old for. On impulse, Leah phoned Nina.

'Sorry,' her mum said, 'Neen's working shifts at the bakery.'

Leah left no message. It looked like another evening of telly and daydreams. Fighting boredom, she went to the shop at the corner of her street for chocolate. She'd read somewhere that eating enough chocolate gave women a feeling similar to an orgasm. She wondered how many *Fuse* bars *that* would require.

There was a familiar face at the counter of the shop.

Iain Foster was buying a copy of the *Ministry Of Sound* magazine.

'Hi,' she said, joining him by the till. Iain was heavily tanned.

'Hi, Leah. Having a good summer?'

'I'm getting a bit bored, to be honest. How about you?'

'Just come back from Ibiza. Had a brilliant time. I'm picking up the photos later on. Maybe you'd like to see them, hear a few of my new sounds?'

'Um, yeah. Why not?' she replied. It was the best offer she'd had all summer. Leah knew, of course, that Iain had asked Meg out. But Meg was away, and hadn't said yes to Iain anyhow. It was also true that Iain had been out with Zoe, not to mention several of the best-looking girls in last year's Year Eleven. According to all the evidence, he was way out of Leah's league.

They arranged to meet the following evening.

9

Jack and Harper's first date – if you could call it that – had been a success. His parents and brother had stayed out of the way all evening. They'd watched the film and some of the extra scenes, then talked about it for a while before Harper's dad came to pick her up. This was the first time that Jack had been out with a girl his own age. You didn't go out with girls in your year at school (not unless you were Iain Foster, anyhow). It was hard to explain why. Something to do with them having known you since you were a kid. Mainly it was because they preferred older blokes. Especially ones with jobs and cars.

It was hard to tell how interested Harper was. At the end of the evening, she'd given him nothing. Not even a kiss on the cheek. It was her dad arriving, he supposed. You weren't going to kiss a bloke when your dad was outside. But Jack wasn't sure that he'd set the right tone. He hadn't shown Harper he was interested in her body as well as her mind. But he had a second chance. This afternoon, he was playing her at table tennis. There was a table you could use at the church she went to. *I know*, she'd said when he raised his eyebrows at the mention of a church hall, *but I'm new here*. The hall was empty. Nobody his age went to church any more, or anywhere associated with it. But he knew the place.

'They used to have discos in here for under fourteens,' he told her.

'They still do. Did you go to any?'

'Just once. It was excruciating. Lots of giggly girls, and lads who weren't really sure why they were there.'

'Including you?'

'Yeah, I guess. The whole thing finished at nine, I remember that. I had to wait till the end because my mum insisted on collecting me. Horrible.'

'Why don't we play? Unless you'd prefer to dance.'

On the table tennis table, Jack saw a different Harper. She hit the ball hard, using plenty of spin, which he found difficult to cope with.

'Who do you normally play with?' he asked, after she'd won the first game convincingly, 21-11.

'My brother. He's younger than you, but he's faster.'

'Thanks a lot.'

'I bet you'll improve, with practice.'

'I've got the time if you have.'

The games became increasingly fierce. They'd played six before Jack actually won one.

'Let's take a break,' Harper said afterwards.

They sat down together, Jack making sure that he was right up against her, even though they were both steaming.

'I really like you,' he said, looking ahead, rather than at her.

'I like you too,' Harper replied and Jack risked putting his arm round her shoulder. She let him. They looked at each other. Harper had a sort of amused look. Jack wasn't sure what it meant, but it was good enough for him. He kissed her.

'That was the sweatiest kiss I've ever had,' Harper said, when they broke apart. 'Want another game?'

He wanted to kiss her again, but said, 'Why not?'

This time, she thrashed him by her biggest score of the day.

'That last one, did you let me win?' he asked.

'Would you have dared kiss me if you'd lost six out of six?'

'I guess not. Shall we call it a day?'

'Fine by me.'

They kissed again. This time, they were interrupted by the arrival of the vicar. She acted as though she hadn't seen anything.

'Sorry, I didn't realise that there was anyone in here. Hello, Harper. How are you getting on? I see you've made a new friend.'

Harper blushed crimson, but then recovered. 'Jack's going to the sixth form college next month, like me. We're on some of the same courses.'

'That's nice. How's Ross getting on? I haven't seen him in a while.'

'He's fine.'

'Ross?' Jack asked, when the vicar was gone.

'The brother I told you about.' She looked at her watch. 'I'd better get going. I'll need a shower before dinner.'

'I'll walk you home.'

'Don't be daft, you live in the opposite direction.'

'I want to,' Jack said, insistently.

Harper kissed him. 'Don't crowd me. I like you. I'll be your girlfriend if you want. But I like to take things a step at a time. Is that OK?'

'It's absolutely brilliant,' Jack said, and kissed her again, but not for too long this time, in case that counted as 'crowding' her.

'What are you doing a week on Saturday?' Harper asked at the door.

'Not a lot,' Jack told her.

'My parents are going away for the weekend,'

Harper said, 'but I think I might be able to persuade them to let me stay behind. Maybe you'd like to come round?'

'You bet.' It was all Jack could do to stop himself punching the air.

'Are you all right?'

'Yeah.' Leah rolled away from Iain and slid her knickers back on. 'It wasn't quite like I expected, that's all.'

'First time's always a bit strange. The second time you'll like it more.'

Iain was fed up of sleeping with virgins. Leah was the seventh girl he'd had to break-in. It always took them a while to know what they were doing and, by then, he was usually bored with them.

'Don't flatter yourself,' she said, tossing the condom into the bin (from where he'd have to remove it before his mum cleaned the bedroom), then donning her vest top. 'There won't *be* a second time.'

'Why? I'm not the bastard everyone says, am I?' Iain didn't mind if Leah thought he was a complete bastard. In some ways, it would make things easier. When he went out with a girl, he wasn't interested in a long-term relationship. That was like getting married. Iain was interested in getting his end away. The quicker the better. Tonight Leah hadn't needed any pressure, just a little encouragement. The way she'd behaved, he'd been surprised when it turned out to be her first time. Now she came over and kissed him on the forehead.

'It's not you,' she reassured him. 'It's me.' This was the line he always used. 'Don't worry about it.'

Leah was picking up her bag. 'You've got a great arse,' he said, because she had. 'If you ever change your mind.'

'I won't,' Leah told him. 'See you, tiger.'

Iain didn't get up. He was still bollock-naked and he couldn't work out what had gone wrong. He'd thought a thing with Leah would tide him over for the ten days until he started sixth form college. Then there would be all those girls from other schools to get to know. His reputation went before him, but most girls still had to find out for themselves. There was also Megan Rhys-Carter, thousands of miles away, but on a possible promise. Wasn't Leah a big buddy of hers? He hoped that wouldn't make any difference.

Iain knew women and he knew what was going on. He wasn't Leah's type any more than she, in the general run of things, was his. She'd used him to lose her cherry. Iain didn't much like being used. But everybody used everybody. What really annoyed him was girls who acted like sex was more than sex. You had to tell it to them straight or they got all clingy. At least Leah wasn't that way.

Iain wondered when Megan got back from Australia.

10

Megan shouldn't have been surprised. Before she went on holiday, four of her gang were still virgins. Now it was down to three. On the first day back, Leah announced that she, too, had succumbed. It was a bloke she'd met on holiday.

'So your week in Cornwall wasn't a complete washout, then?' Meg asked.

'I didn't want to be the last one,' Leah told her, in a low voice. 'I just wanted to get the whole thing over with. Don't you feel like that sometimes?'

'Sometimes,' Megan said. 'But I'm going to wait for someone special.'

'Someone like Iain Foster?' Beth teased.

'He'll have all those sixth form girls at the college to go after,' Megan said. 'I don't think he'll be interested in me.'

'You can do better than him,' Leah said, which surprised Meg a little.

'Go on then, tell us all about this lad on holiday,' Beth ordered Leah.

'There's not a lot to tell. We had some drinks. We did it on a beach. It was over pretty quickly,' Leah said.

'Do you think boys last longer as they get older?' Bethany asked, and Megan began to feel excluded.

'Tell us about Australia,' Leah said, and, gratefully, Megan did.

It was weird, after school, to get off the bus two stops earlier and make the short walk to Joe's. Since getting back from Sydney, three days before, Meg had hardly begun adjusting to her new home. During the day, she'd done little but sleep. Her longest conversation with Joe had been at three in the morning. It was the day after her return. She'd woken from a deep sleep and showered before going to the kitchen for something to eat. There was noise coming from the living room, so she'd looked in. Joe was stretched out on the sofa watching telly. He had an overflowing ash-tray and several empty lager bottles by his side. Seeing Meg, he'd asked if she wanted a drink.

'No thanks. I've only just woken up.'

'You're going to have a long day, then. I know what I was like when I came back from visiting Pat and Sarah that year they were living in Melbourne. Do you remember that?'

'No,' Meg confessed. 'I was too young.'

'Had a great time. But it took me a week to get over the jet-lag when we got home. Your best bet is to stay up from now on, resist sleep at all costs and get an early night tomorrow . . . I mean today.'

'I'll do my best.'

Joe went to bed when his programme – a documentary about whales – was over. He had all the satellite channels, so Meg flicked through them until seven, when it began to get light. Then she went for a run. Her five weeks in Australia had made her more conscious of the need to stay fit. She felt cheated though. Over there, it had been winter. Here, summer had come and gone during her absence. She had no tan, nothing much to show for her holiday except slightly improved muscle tone. More annoying, she'd had her mobile switched on all the time since she'd got back and Iain Foster *still* hadn't phoned.

That night, Meg managed to keep going until nine, then slept until six. She'd woken at six today, as well. It was too early and now she was knackered from school. Maybe if she took a catnap . . . Rather than unlocking the gate at the side and descending the steps to the flat's separate entrance, Megan went in by the front door. Joe called from upstairs.

'Meg, is that you? Put the kettle on, would you?'

'How was your day?' he asked, when she took two

mugs of tea up to his office. He had shaved, she was pleased to see. She hated the patchy ginger beard he got when he forgot for a few days. It reminded Meg of her own auburn hair, which didn't come from Sarah's family.

'Same old, same old,' she said. 'At least I managed to stay awake.'

'That's something. What do you want to eat tonight?'

'Whatever. I thought I'd take a little nap then have a shower.'

'OK. Don't sleep too long. I'll order Chinese.'

Megan tried, but couldn't sleep. Maybe that was for the best. She decided to have a bath, which would relax her. The bathroom was next to Joe's study. She popped her head in to tell him what she was doing, but he'd gone out. Five minutes later, she got into the bath. Within minutes of the heat hitting her, she was fast out, head propped against the porcelain, feet pushed up against the edge beneath the taps. She didn't hear Joe come back. The next sound she heard was the toilet flushing. The bathroom door opened. As Joe walked in, Meg let out a yelp. He swore.

'I'm sorry. I didn't . . .'

'Don't be daft.' Megan sat up quickly so that her knees covered her chest, splashing water all over the bathroom floor. 'You didn't know I was in here.'

Joe hurried out.

When Meg got back from school the next day, somebody had fitted a lock to the inside of the bathroom door.

'I met him,' Parvinder told the others when they were round at Zoe's on Wednesday evening.

'Met who?' That was Leah, first with the obvious question.

'The guy I'm going to marry.'

'Hold on,' Zoe said. 'Before you went to Pakistan for the summer, you told me that they wouldn't marry you off to some farm boy who doesn't speak English. Do you mean to say . . . ?'

'He was born here,' Parvinder interrupted. 'He was in Pakistan for the summer holidays, like me.'

'What's he called?' Meg asked.

'Sanjeev. He only lives ten miles away. We're going to meet up.'

'How old is he?' Beth asked.

'Seventeen. He's going to university next year if he gets the grades, so it looks like Mum and Dad will be happy for me to go, too. Then, by the time I graduate, he should have a job and we can get married. Or maybe we'll get married before then. Nothing's definite, except that it's him and me.'

'And you're *happy* about that?' Nina asked, incredulous.

It was interesting, Parvinder thought, to see her friends' reactions. Zoe was reserved, concerned that Parvinder wasn't being forced into anything. Bethany looked happy, the way any friend might be when you'd just announced your engagement. Nina looked edgy. There were probably all sorts of reasons for this. She and Parvinder had never been terribly close. Also Nina and Tom, with their plans to live together, would be upstaged by Parvinder getting married.

The ones whose reactions Parvinder couldn't predict were Leah and Meg. Usually, but not always, Leah followed Meg's lead. Meg asked a question.

'What's he like? I mean, did you speak to him or did you just see him?'

'I spoke to him. It's not the middle ages over there. He's from a Sikh background, like me. Not a strict Sikh, but he takes it seriously, the way I do.'

'How do you know this?' Zoe asked.

'We weren't meant to be left alone together, but we were.'

'Did you . . . do anything?' Leah asked.

'A little. We talked and . . . one time, we kissed.'

'Tongues?' Nina.

Parvinder giggled and nodded.

'Is he good-looking?' Beth.

'I think so.'

'Are his family well-off?' Zoe.

'His dad's a solicitor. Sanjeev's the eldest son.'

'Are you in love with him?' Beth.

'Not yet,' Parvinder said. 'But I will be.'

On Thursday evening, Leah arranged to see Meg. Anxious, she got there early. She went straight to the flat, knocking on the outside door, then had to wait while Megan came down from Joe's part of the house.

'I was eating with Joe,' she explained.

'I thought you'd be cooking for yourself,' Leah said.

'There's a kettle and a microwave but it's not a proper kitchen.'

'Is Joe a good cook?' Leah asked.

'He's good at ordering takeouts and paying for them. I cooked tonight.'

'Very domestic.'

Meg's mobile rang. 'Scuse me,' she said. Her face lit up when she heard who it was. Leah listened.

'No, it's OK,' Meg was saying. 'I'm glad you called. I guess I could. Where? All right. Quarter to eight. Bye.'

She hung up. 'Iain Foster's asked me out on Saturday night.'

'Cool.' Leah sounded unconvincing, even to her own ears. 'Where?'

'In town. We'll decide what to do when we meet.'

'Probably back to his for a couple of drinks and a shag.'

'Pardon?' Meg sounded offended and Leah regretted what she'd just said.

'That's Iain's main technique,' she explained. 'He has the house to himself most Saturday nights and he makes the most of it.'

'And you know this because . . . ?'

Leah started to say it was common knowledge, but it wasn't, not really, and she had come round specifically to tell Megan, in case Iain did ask her out again.

'I lied to you and Beth on the bus. There was no boy in Cornwall. Iain chatted me up in a shop. I went round to his one Saturday.'

'You went out with Iain?' Meg sounded shocked, as well she should.

'Not as in *going out with*,' Leah explained. 'I just went there the once.'

'You *knew* that he'd asked me out.'

'Don't give me a hard time, Meg. I was lonely. I couldn't ask you and it wasn't as if you were actually going out with him.'

'But how could you have sex with him!'

'It's not that big a deal.' Leah felt her face flush as she tried to defend herself. 'I mean, me and how many others? Iain's the male equivalent of Tracey Cook. You do realise that?'

'Thanks very much for bringing her up.' Meg looked really angry and Leah regretted coming round. Iain would never have told Megan what happened. Why had Leah felt the need to kiss-and-tell?

'Maybe I'd better go,' she said. Meg immediately calmed down.

'You only just got here. I'm sorry. I know what Iain's like, but I've been waiting for him to ring, then he does and before I can take it in you come out with . . . why didn't you tell me before?'

Leah wasn't sure of the answer, but did her best. 'Because I knew you were interested in him. Because it wasn't about who I did it with, it was about doing it. I just wanted to get it over with.'

There was an awkward silence.

'Do you want some coffee?' Without waiting for an answer, Megan put the kettle on. Leah tried to come up with a new topic of conversation.

'This'd be a great place for a party,' she said.

'A small party. It's just a bedsit, really.' Meg changed the subject back to Iain. 'Did he get you drunk, or stoned, or something?' When Leah didn't reply, she added, 'I'm going out with him on Saturday. You owe me an answer. *Why* did you do it with him?'

Leah hesitated, then told the truth. 'To find out if I liked it.'

Megan frowned. 'And did you?'

'Not much.'

'Maybe,' Meg said, handing Leah a mug, 'you didn't like it much because you were with the wrong person. Maybe it'd be different if you were in love.'

'I'm sure it would,' Leah said. 'But I needed to find out.'

'You said that before,' Megan told her. 'But it doesn't make sense. I mean, I want to find out too. But that doesn't mean I'm going to do it with the first presentable person who asks me. Not even Iain Foster, unless it feels right.'

She wants to fall in love with him, Leah thought. But Iain was a stupid person to choose to fall in love with. He was a user, which was why Leah had used him. Though maybe, only a thin maybe, Megan could change him.

'He was OK with me,' Leah added, kindly. 'Nice. Gentle, even.'

'But he didn't want to see you again?'

'He might have done. I told him afterwards: it wasn't him, it was me.'

'And how did he take that?'

'Fine.'

Megan stared out of the window, as though still struggling to take it all in. Then she seemed to remember that Leah was a close friend and her tone changed.

'Did it hurt much?'

'Not much.'

'But it wasn't . . . ?'

'I'm trying to forget about it,' Leah said. 'It wasn't anything. To be honest, I'm trying to pretend it never happened.'

'I only wanted to know—'

Irritated now, Leah resorted to sarcasm. 'Tell you what, why don't you sleep with him Saturday? Then we can compare notes.'

Meg looked offended. Leah apologised. 'I don't know what I'm on about. Ignore me. I only went with him because . . .' But she couldn't put the real reason into words. 'I didn't want to be last,' she said, finally.

'Nobody does,' Meg said. 'But someone always has to be.'

11

Zoe and Nina only had one class together: Maths. It was Zoe's worst subject. She should get the grade she needed, but would have to work hard. It hurt, not being in a top group. Nina, by contrast, *should* be in a top group, but wasn't. Teachers tended to underestimate her because she was loud and liked to gossip.

On Thursday night, she and Zoe were working together on an assignment. Nina was doing most of the thinking. In Maths, everything was supposed to have a right or wrong answer. Yet Zoe knew that, if they handed in identical work, she would get the higher mark. The Maths teacher, Mr Jones, liked her a lot.

'Do you think every bloke who fancies you automatically imagines having sex with you?' Nina asked.

'I don't like to think about that,' Zoe said.

'I saw Johnny Jones trying to sneak a look down your blouse when he was helping you today.'

'Nina! God, even if he did, I wouldn't want to know about it.'

'He's pretty fit.'

'He must be thirty. I don't fancy him at all. And teachers aren't supposed to . . . the thought makes me puke.'

'So who *doesn't* make you puke?' Nina left a pause. 'Iain Foster?'

'That didn't work out.'

'Because you wouldn't go all the way on the first date.'

'Something like that. He was really . . . I don't like talking about this.'

Nina didn't let Zoe get away with that one. 'If you can't talk about it with me,' she said, 'how are you ever going to talk about it with a boy?'

She had a point, Zoe realised. Looking away from Nina, she tried to tell her about it. 'After Jack and Meg went upstairs, he was really flattering and told me how great I was and how intelligent and how he wasn't only interested in me for my looks and it had taken him months to work up the courage to ask me out. Then we fooled around a bit and I let him go further than I usually do.'

'*Usually*? How many proper boyfriends have you had?'

'Three. If you count Iain, which I don't. Except . . .' Zoe wondered how to put this. Nina was right. She ought to talk it over with someone. Parvinder would be the obvious choice, but Nina was the one with the experience. 'So before I know it, I'm out of my dress and Iain's down to his boxer shorts and that's when I tell him: *no chance.*'

'How did he take it?'

'All right. He didn't try to pressure me. We made out for a while. Then he gave me this spiel about how once a guy got excited it was really hard to turn it off.'

'Bullshit!' Nina interrupted.

'He sounded so convincing. Then he asked me to . . .' Embarrassed, Zoe whispered the words to Nina.

'*Cheeky!*' Nina said. 'Tom only gets that if he's been really, really nice.'

'And I tried, but I just couldn't do it. Then I got embarrassed, and asked Iain to leave and, suddenly, he started acting all stroppy, like a stranger. Five minutes later, he was gone and I felt like, what? A tease, maybe. A silly prude.'

'You've got nothing to feel bad about,' Nina told her. 'Iain's a user, everybody knows that. I was surprised you even went out with him.'

'I'm surprised, too,' Zoe said. 'But everyone I know fancies him.'

'I don't,' Nina said. 'He's too smarmy, too full of himself.'

'Whatever. I can't stand the sight of him now. But I was still flattered he asked me. He's not been out with a girl in our year before.'

'You'll find someone better,' Nina urged.

Zoe was doubtful. They returned to the Maths, which Nina cleared in no time, explaining some tricky points in the process.

'You're really sharp,' Zoe said. 'I don't understand why you aren't going to do 'A' levels.'

'I don't know what I'd do with 'A' levels,' Nina said.

'Go to university, I guess.'

'You think I'm bright enough?'

'Of course you are. If you worked at it. I mean, you're still doing a couple of nights at the bakery, aren't you? That must get in the way.'

'Yeah,' Nina said. 'I want to have some money for next year, when Tom and I get a flat. But I don't want to close off my options.'

'How does Tom feel about you going to uni?' Zoe asked.

'We've not discussed it. I expect he'd think I'd be wasting my time.'

Zoe wasn't sure what to say. She knew better than to be rude about Tom.

'He might be worried about losing you,' she suggested.

'Yeah,' Nina agreed. 'That's probably all it is. If there was a university round here, maybe he'd be all right with it. But we're in the middle of nowhere.'

'There are always weekends.'

'Tom wants more than weekends. So do I.' Outside, a car sounded its horn. 'That'll be him now. Gotta go.'

Nina rushed off. It was funny, Zoe thought: the rest of the gang envied Nina's relationship with Tom, but Zoe didn't. She didn't envy her at all.

On Saturday night, Iain met Megan at The Roxy in town. The Roxy was an old place and still had 'love' seats, nearly double the usual size. Close contact heightened expectation, allowing Iain to put an unobtrusive, affectionate arm around her. The film, however, sucked. Afterwards, without any prompting, Megan invited him back to hers. This threw Iain a little.

'My parents'll be out until late and my sister's on a sleepover, so it might be cooler to go back to mine.'

'Do you mind if we don't?' Megan said. 'Thing is, I'm staying at my godfather's and this is the first Saturday night I've been out. He'll worry. It's a great place. I've got my own flat, TV and everything.'

Iain liked the sound of that flat. They caught a bus to

her godfather's, which he calculated was a four mile walk or an eight quid taxi back to his. But maybe he'd be welcome to stay the night. Megan's parents were pretty unconventional, so her godfather might be, too.

When Iain walked in, Joe waved casually. He was smoking a roll-up and looked like a *Big Issue* seller: bad haircut, shapeless jeans and an ancient Nirvana T-shirt. Joe offered Iain a beer, which he accepted. When he got up, Iain saw that he used a walking stick. Poor sod. It was probably months since he got laid.

Joe had satellite TV and let Iain choose a channel. He went for MTV Dance, which was full of muscular black women wearing next to nothing. He could tell, though, that Megan wasn't keen. She looked hot tonight, in a leather skirt, purple top and sheer black stockings. Or were they tights? He'd find out soon enough.

'Are you going to show me this basement flat?' he asked her.

'If you're sure you've seen enough of Destiny's Child,' Megan said.

It was exactly as she'd promised: double bed, with her own TV, stereo and shower. This was going to be like having a girlfriend with her own place, at least until Meg's parents got back. Whatever. Christmas was three months away. Iain's girlfriends never lasted that long.

* * *

Tom got out of bed and lit a cigarette. Nina didn't like it when he smoked, especially in the bedroom. She hated her sheets to smell of smoke. He began to talk about how much money they'd got saved.

'I've been looking at prices. A flat in town can set you back much more than a hundred quid a week. But there are villages a few miles out where you can rent a two-bed house for three hundred a month.'

'A house?' Nina said. 'What would we want with a whole house? Both of us have lived in flats all our lives.'

'Don't you want better?' Tom squeezed her shoulder.

'Course I do. But I want to be somewhere where I can see my friends, not some old ruin surrounded by fields with a bus that only comes twice a day.'

'You can learn to drive. Until then, I'll take you everywhere.'

'How am I ever going to afford a car on my wages at the bakery?'

'We'll work something out.'

'Yeah, course we will.'

She heard Mum coming in from the pub. Tonight she'd meant to tell Tom about her change of plan. But it could wait, at least until she was sure. He'd support her, she knew he would. When he got used to the idea.

It might take a while. Hurriedly, she dressed, then the two of them joined Mum for a brew.

Megan was tempted, but not tempted enough.

'What's wrong?' Iain said. His trousers had somehow ended up around his ankles. She had never seen an erect penis before, except in a photo. It wasn't ugly, as she'd feared. Not threatening, exactly. She was sure she could get used to it. In time. At this moment, however, Meg was daunted by the thought of having it anywhere near her.

'Nothing's wrong,' she reassured him. 'But you're hurrying me. This is a first date, remember? Let's get dressed, go see Joe. He has some great DVDs.'

Iain hesitated, but she was already standing, fastening her bra. Grumpily, he got out of bed and, with his back to her, began to dress.

'What's Joe doing in on a Saturday night?' Iain asked. 'Doesn't he have a . . . y'know . . . social life?'

'Sure,' Meg replied. 'But lots of people stay in on Saturday night.'

'What's with his leg?' Iain asked. 'Why does he use a stick?'

'A childhood injury,' Meg told him.

'He needs to smarten himself up,' Iain said, turning

round as he buttoned his flies. 'Or he'll never get a girlfriend.'

'He has girlfriends,' Meg lied, then wondered why she'd felt the need to.

'But not at the moment, right?' Iain said.

'Right,' Meg said, tickling her new boyfriend under the chin. 'Maybe you could give him some pointers. You seem to have lots of experience.'

Iain chuckled, and they kissed. He was such a great kisser, moist, but not too moist, his tongue making her think of what they'd nearly done and wishing that now, right now, they were doing it. Meg pulled away, determined that she wasn't going to be another notch on his bed post, a one-night-stand, like Leah.

It was Jack's first visit to Harper's house, which was three times the size of his. Her brother was in, but both of her parents were away, visiting relatives. Jack was impressed that they trusted her enough to leave her in the house on her own.

'They don't know you're coming,' Harper said. 'I haven't said much about you. When the time comes, I'll introduce you as someone I met at college rather than this guy who picked me up in the library.'

'Have they met any of your boyfriends before?' Jack asked.

'Only the one who went to the same church as us,' Harper said. 'They thought he was great. Unfortunately, I didn't agree.'

Jack laughed. He wasn't religious, but it didn't bother him that Harper was.

'Do you want to see my room?' she asked.

'Sure.' This was a big moment for Jack, the first time he'd been invited into a girl's bedroom. He'd never made it past Meg's front door (and going into Zoe's room with her hardly counted). He'd been in Nina's council flat and met her mum, Pauline, who looked like her older sister. But – perhaps because Pauline was there – they hadn't moved from the living room to Nina's bedroom. Jack didn't know what to expect. Or what was expected of him.

The room was bigger than the one which Jack shared with his brother. There was a framed Matisse poster, some photographs of friends and family, a TV, video and a stereo. Luxury. The single bed had a plain grey duvet covering it.

'Do you want to choose some music?'

He looked through the CDs, which were less embarrassing than he might have feared, and picked the latest Charlatans. Then he joined Harper on the bed.

'What do you think?'

'It's nice. I like it.'

He kissed her gently, unsure how far to go or how fast. With Meg, all he'd got was a few kisses and a fumbled grope. Nina had been far more enthusiastic. If he'd had the nerve, and a place to take her, they might have gone all the way. But with Harper, he had no idea. Her tongue explored his mouth. Her hands moved up and down his back. How experienced was she? She was so good-looking, she must have had lots of boyfriends. What if he wasn't up to scratch? She would put up with him being worse than her at table tennis. But if he was bad at sex too . . . He pushed a hand up Harper's top, roughly pushing against the right cup of her bra.

'Take it easy,' she said. 'It's a new one.'

'Then perhaps you'd better take it off,' he ventured.

'All in good time,' she said, and kissed him again.

That was decided then. He would let her set the pace.

12

'What do you want to do for your birthday?' Joe asked Megan.

She was sixteen at the end of the month. It was odd, having such a big birthday without Pat or Sarah around. But they had celebrated early, in Sydney. Her parents might be half a world away, but they talked on the phone all the time. Sarah, in particular, felt guilty about leaving Meg behind. Meg had to keep reassuring her that everything was fine.

'I was thinking of a small party,' Meg replied, 'the following Saturday.'

Her birthday itself was on a Monday – a useless day to do anything. Joe played with his pencil, rolling it between each of the fingers of his right hand.

'How small?' he asked.

'How many would fit in the basement?' she asked. 'Ten? Twelve?'

'Only if you took the bed out.'

'That'd stop anybody getting the wrong idea,' she said.

Joe laughed. 'Seriously,' he said. 'You can have a party upstairs, as long as you keep it to invited guests only. I don't want half your year gatecrashing.'

'I'm not sure I could do that to you,' Meg said. 'You don't know what teenage parties are like.'

Joe raised an eyebrow. 'Don't suppose they've changed much since my time,' he said. 'The carpets need cleaning anyway. We'll cover up the TV and satellite gear. There's not a lot else to break. It's been ages since I had a party here.'

'That's great. You're the best godfather in the world.' Meg hugged Joe, then kissed him. He looked bashful. She realised that he hadn't said anything about going out himself. She didn't know how to put this tactfully.

'What will you do?'

'I'll stay out of sight,' Joe promised. 'I'll probably hang out in my office. That way, I can get some work done and make sure nobody messes with my stuff. Also, I'll be there if you need me.'

'OK,' Megan said. 'That's so cool. Thanks.'

They agreed on a maximum of thirty people. Megan went downstairs to draw up a list. She tried to decide who to tell first, Leah or Iain. She chose Leah.

Mistake.

'All I need,' Leah said, on hearing the news. 'A party to look forward to.'

'Don't worry,' Meg said. 'I'll sort out a selection of single blokes for you.'

'You'd better,' Leah said, without conviction.

Next, Meg rang Parvinder. 'Maybe you could bring Sanjeev,' she said. 'Or will he have already gone off to university?'

'He doesn't go until the weekend after,' Parvinder said. Sanjeev had got the grades he needed to do Law, as his father had before him. 'But I'm not sure either set of parents would be happy about us seeing each other at a teenage party.'

'You mean you need a chaperone?'

'Not exactly . . . I'll tell him about it.'

Zoe wasn't sure if she could make it. 'I'm meant to be going to this dance event with Mum and Dad. I'll try to get out of it, only . . .'

'It's my sixteenth,' Meg reminded her.

'And I'll come. But I might have to show up late. Iain's going to be there, I take it?'

'I haven't rung him yet.'

'But the two of you are going out?'

'Yes,' Megan said, though she and Iain hadn't exactly put their relationship into those words. 'We are.'

Zoe said nothing but an unspoken question hung in the air. Meg answered it.

'He never talks about you. Or any girl he's been out

with, for that matter. I tease him a little about all his exes. I'm sure he'll be fine around you. Bring a date, if you're worried. You're always spoilt for choice.'

'Not lately,' Zoe said. 'OK. I'll try to make it. Should be fun.'

Nobody else had anything on. After a few more calls, Meg did a head count. She was at least three boys down. Hesitantly, she rang Jack Green. Jack would be just right for Leah. And he got on with Zoe, if it came to that.

Jack sounded surprised to hear from Meg. 'Your sixteenth. Sure, I'd love to come. OK if I bring someone?'

'Sure, but only one. I have a limit,' Meg said, then quipped, 'and make sure he's good-looking.'

'He's a she,' Jack said. 'See you a week on Saturday.'

He hung up and Meg cursed. Why had she assumed that Jack would be single? He must have long since got over their failed date. Jack was good-looking in an old-fashioned kind of way. When he was relaxed, he could hold a conversation. True, he wasn't as smooth as Iain. But who was?

Iain! Of course. He would sort the missing men.

'No worries,' he said when she called. 'Just tell me how many you need.'

'I'll get back to you next week when I'm sure how

many girls from school are coming.'

'Fine. And what about the day itself? Can I see you on your birthday?'

'I certainly hope so. Joe's taking me out for a meal. Perhaps you could come round later?'

'It's a date.'

Parvinder rang back. Sanjeev figured he could get to the party, no trouble, as long as they didn't tell their families where he was going. So he couldn't stay at her place. Parvinder wondered whether there was a spare bed he could use.

'Not really,' Meg told her. 'That's where I am.'

'Or a sofa?'

'I can do better than that,' Meg offered. 'He can have my room at home. It's only a fifteen-minute walk from Joe's. Don't tell anyone and I'll give you my key.'

'You're a star,' Parvinder said. 'Thanks.'

Megan sat on the bed and hugged herself. She was turning sixteen. She had a handsome, helpful boyfriend. And she had a party to look forward to.

When Ross didn't show up at the first disco of the autumn term, Beth decided to dismiss what had happened as an aberration, a hallucination even. After all, some of her friends seemed convinced she'd made it up. Sometimes even *she* thought that she had. Beth had seen Ross just once since it happened, walking into church with his parents. He hadn't noticed Bethany, watching from her bedroom window.

On the Sunday before Meg's sixteenth, Beth happened to spot Jack Green hanging around the church gates. What was he doing there? If he wanted to talk to Beth, he only had to ring the vicarage door. Beth was about to go out and see him when the scant group of evening attenders began to leave the service. A tall girl came out and hurried up to Jack. She was rather beautiful, with long, blonde hair, blow-dried to the face. Jack had come for her, not Beth. The couple kissed.

'I saw this girl,' Bethany told Mum over dinner, then described her.

'That would be Harper Simm.'

'Simm?'

'Yes, she's the older sister of that lad who started coming to the discos last term, Ross. Why do you ask?'

'I saw her with a guy I know, that's all,' Beth muttered, taken aback. Without asking, she'd finally found out Ross's surname.

'You mean Jack. Yes, he plays table tennis with her in the hall sometimes. Good-looking lad. Always polite.'

After dinner, Beth looked up Sim and Simm in the

phone book. There was nobody in the right area. But they'd only recently moved in. So she tried directory enquiries and got the number straight away. Now all she had to do was work up the nerve to call him. But she couldn't do it. She rang Nina instead.

'If you want,' her friend offered, 'I'll call him up for you.'

'Oh, that would be just great,' Bethany told her. 'What would you say – *my mate fancies you*? And he'd reply *Yeah I'd kind of worked that out after we did it at the disco two and a half months ago*. I reckon I should just forget it.'

'What's the worst that could happen?' Nina asked. 'A knock-back. But at least you'd know where you stood.'

At school the next day, Beth talked it over with Meg, Zoe, Parvinder and Leah. They divided 50–50 on whether Beth should call Ross. Meg and Parvinder were for, the others against.

'You don't really know him,' Leah pointed out. 'You used him for sex. It's not a good basis for a relationship.'

'Boys don't think about sex that way,' Zoe argued. 'I doubt he feels used. But Leah's right. It's not a good basis for a real relationship. He'll probably think you're offering him a repeat performance.'

'Oh, for God's sake, ring him up!' Meg said. 'You've got nothing to lose, and you might just get some peace of mind.'

'His sister's at college and both his parents work, right?' Parvinder said. 'So time it for when he should have just got in from school and his sister won't be back yet.'

This was the best advice. As soon as she got in from school, before she had time to lose her nerve, Beth did just that. Ross answered on the fourth ring.

'Hi, it's Beth. Remember me?'

'Ummm, yeah. How are you?'

'I'm fine,' Beth said, leaving space for an apology which didn't come. She swallowed her pride. 'I wanted to ask you a favour,' she said.

'Uh, sure.'

'My friend's having this party on Saturday, her sixteenth, but she's short of lads. I said I'd try and find a few to make up the numbers.'

'Oh,' Ross said, non-committally. 'Right.'

'Also, it would be nice to see you again. I enjoyed . . .' Beth didn't know what to say she'd enjoyed, so stumbled on. 'I hoped . . .'

'I wanted to call you,' Ross said. 'But your dad's my teacher. And your mum . . .'

'I know,' Beth said. 'I thought it might be something

like that. But I'd still like to see you again. You don't have to come to the house. I could give you Meg's address.'

'Did you say it was her *sixteenth* birthday party? She's older than you.'

'By a few months,' Beth said.

'Right.' Ross still sounded very unsure of himself.

'Will you come?'

'I'll see if I can make it,' Ross said.

Bethany gave him her mobile number and said goodbye.

'I think he's just shy,' Beth told Megan on the bus into school the following day, Meg's birthday. They had the back of the bus to themselves.

'Is his sister *really* good-looking?' Meg asked.

'Really. Jack seemed keen on her. He must be, waiting for her like that.'

'Good,' Megan said. 'I'm glad he's found someone. I was a bit off with him when we went out.'

'Why?'

'Dunno.' Meg thought about it for a moment. 'I was jealous of Zoe being with Iain and Jack couldn't match up to him. It didn't matter how nice he was.'

'Jack's much nicer than Iain,' Bethany said.

'How can you know that?'

'*D'oh!* He just is. Iain's a stereotype. A smooth-tongued, well-off, handsome bastard – and proud of it. Jack's a good-looking, well-meaning guy.'

'Are you criticising me?' Megan asked, not in a hurt way.

'Hardly. Everyone wants to be seen on the arm of the best-looking guy in town. But you're not going to end up with him, because you know he'll cheat on you and, anyhow, he's not the kind of guy you really want to end up with.'

'I'm not thinking about *ending up* with anyone,' Megan said. 'But tell me, if he's so bad, why am I going out with him?'

'I'll bet he's brilliant in bed,' Bethany said.

To Bethany's surprise, Meg blushed. 'What did I say?' Bethany asked in a lowered voice. 'I mean, it's nothing to be embarrassed about. We've all talked about it before. Ever since Year Eight, you've had it in mind that Iain Foster would be the first bloke you did it with. And now you have.'

To Bethany's surprise, Megan gave the smallest shake of her head.

'But you've been seeing him for three weeks!' Beth hissed.

'I want to be sure. Maybe I will be when he comes over tonight.'

'He's on a promise?'

'More like a hint,' Meg said.

'And he hasn't pressured you?'

'He has a bit,' Megan confessed. 'But he's had lots of other girls, so he can damn well wait for me. I need to be sure that he's for real, that he won't dump me as soon as he's got what he wants.'

'Good for you,' Bethany said. 'Keep him dangling. Follow the rules.'

'It's not *The Rules*,' Megan said. 'I don't want to marry him when I'm older. I don't want to be just another conquest, either. I want us to be . . . equals.'

Meg got off the bus just as Beth's mobile rang. She looked at the number. Ross. He was ringing her the moment he got in from school. That was sweet.

'The party on Saturday,' he said. 'I don't think it's a good idea.'

'You could bring a couple of friends if you—'

'No, I really don't think so.'

'Is it because your sister's going?' Beth asked, the thought having just occurred to her.

'Harper's going? She's in the sixth form.'

'Yes, but she's going out with this guy Meg used to date.'

'I've got to go,' Ross said, abruptly, and hung up.

13

There was only one smart restaurant in town and on a Monday night it was dead. Joe's hair was newly cut. He'd bought a silk shirt for the occasion and ironed his best pair of jeans. He'd even polished his one good pair of shoes.

'Looking the way you do today,' Megan said, 'you'd make some woman a good catch.'

'The way that waitress keeps giving me the evil eye, she thinks I already have.'

Meg was dressed to kill (for Iain later, not Joe) and was showing much more cleavage than was common in Middleton on a Monday. Meg glanced at the waitress, a thirtyish brunette wearing too much mascara. She half raised her hand.

'Can I help you?' the woman said, disdain clear in her voice.

She put on her little girl voice. 'An ash-tray for my dad, please.'

Meg enjoyed the waitress's double take. Hurriedly,

she got the ash-tray.

'We're in the no smoking section,' Joe pointed out.

'There's nobody to complain,' Meg said. 'Go on, have one. Relax.'

After Joe had lit up and downed an inch of wine, he said, 'You've never called me that before.'

'What?' Megan asked, though she knew what he meant.

'Your dad.'

'Sorry. Couldn't resist. I wanted to see the look on her face.'

'It was a beaut, wasn't it?' They both had a laugh, but Megan knew she'd ducked his question, and that wasn't fair.

'Anyhow,' she said, 'you are, aren't you?'

'How do you mean?'

'My dad.'

Joe looked uncomfortable. 'We've never really talked about it,' he said.

'We're talking now,' Meg said, as Joe smoked most of his cigarette in one go. He had a big slurp of wine before speaking again.

'When Pat asked me and I agreed, they said I could have as much or as little contact with you as I wanted. I had no obligation. If I moved away or married and it turned out I didn't have time for you, that was fine.'

'But you've never done either.'

Joe shook his head ruefully. 'Never met the right person.'

'You could have moved somewhere more exciting. Middleton suits Pat and Sarah, but it's hardly Manchester or London.'

'I can work anywhere. Housing was cheap when I came here.'

'We came,' Meg reminded him. 'You followed.'

'That's right,' Joe told her. 'I did.'

'Because of me?' she asked, not sure she wanted the responsibility which came with the answer.

'Because of Pat and Sarah, too. But mainly because of you. I wanted to be around, to see you grow up. Which you have, magnificently.'

Their starter came. The waitress became chatty. 'Just catch my eye if you need anything. A special occasion, is it?'

'Sixteenth birthday.'

'They grow quickly, don't they?' The waitress winked at Joe. 'You don't look old enough.'

'That's right. I'm not.'

'She likes you,' Meg said, when the woman was gone. 'You might have a chance there.'

'Not my type,' Joe said, spearing a prawn.

Meg decided to risk a question which several of her

friends had asked her. 'It isn't that you . . . prefer blokes, is it?'

Joe grinned. 'Tried it once, didn't like it.'

'Don't be offended.'

'I'm not. My best mate Eddie's gay. So it's natural some people assume . . .'

'Only I can't remember you ever having a serious girlfriend.'

'I've had a serious girlfriend,' Joe told her. 'But it was a long time ago and it still hurts to talk about it. Maybe your birthday isn't the time to rake it all up.'

They ate in silence for a couple of minutes.

'I'm glad you're my dad,' Meg said softly. 'Most people in my situation, their father's anonymous, a sperm donor.'

'That's all I was, really.'

'Come *on*. These days, you can buy sperm off the internet. I'm having dinner with a real person, one I look like.'

'Not too much, thank God,' Joe said, as the waitress came to take away their plates, flashing Meg's father another flirtatious smile as she did so.

Iain liked cycling. It kept him in shape and it got him around. He was adept at avoiding cars. You had to watch out for drunken drivers on some of these narrow lanes, but he never wore a helmet. They looked sissy and, anyhow, he liked the feel of the wind in his hair.

September was sliding into October and the evening was blissfully mild. Iain had a book of poetry in one pocket and a soul love songs CD in the other, Meg's birthday present. He was practically on a promise tonight. It was over a month since he'd been with Leah, the longest he'd gone without a shag since losing it, aged fourteen and three quarters, to a girl two years older.

Meg's godfather's house was in one of the cheaper parts of town. Meg hadn't been precise about when she'd be back from her meal. There were no lights on. Luckily, as Iain was thinking he'd got there too early, a taxi pulled up.

'You can bring that inside if you want,' Joe said, pointing at Iain's bike.

'Thanks. I'm sure it'll be safe here,' Iain told him, locking it to a drain pipe. He didn't want to talk to Joe when he collected his bike, not after what he and Meg would have been up to. She stepped out of the car, big smile on her face.

'You look fantastic,' he said, without exaggeration.

'So do you.' Meg was a little drunk, he could tell.

'Let me get you a beer,' Joe said, ushering Iain into the hall.

'Just Coke for me,' Meg said, following Iain in. She kissed him, resting both hands on his buttocks, even though Joe was only a few feet away.

Joe brought the drinks. He looked smart, not as nerd-like as usual, and a fleeting suspicion crept across Iain's mind.

'I need to check my e-mail,' Joe said. 'I'm doing some work for a mag in California and they're eight hours behind. I'll see you guys later.'

'We'll be downstairs,' Meg said. She took Iain's hand and led him down into the basement flat. Once there, they kissed hungrily. Iain almost forgot to give Meg her presents, they got so carried away. She was delighted with them. He put the CD on, then they returned to the bed. Iain was reaching for his condoms when Meg pulled away.

'Sorry,' she said. 'Cramp in my ankle.'

Iain made conversation as she rubbed it. 'Where did Joe take you tonight?'

She told him. A place his parents went for wedding anniversaries.

'I'm surprised Joe can afford a place like that,' Iain said.

'Why? He's always busy with work.'

'Pay OK, do they, his funny drawings?'

'I guess. He'd bought a new shirt, too. Did you notice? Designer label.'

117

'Or a good knock-off,' Iain said. 'Hey, you don't think he's got the horn for you, do you? I mean, you're not a little girl any more.'

'He's my *godfather*, for crying out loud.'

'So? He's a single bloke with all his own teeth and hair. He might think he's in with a chance.'

Meg tickled him under the chin. 'You're not a wee bit jealous of him taking me out, are you?'

They kissed, but when he put his hand under her skirt, she moved it away.

'There's no need to worry about Joe. He's more than a godfather, if you really want to know. Otherwise Pat and Sarah wouldn't have left me with him.'

'How do you mean?' Iain knew he'd made a mistake before the question was out of his mouth. There was an art to conversation when you wanted to seduce someone. You could go so far in finding out about them, but when the topic became serious, it was imperative that you switched back to flirtation, flattery. He'd left it too late. Now, out spilled Meg's secrets: the lesbian lovers who wanted a child, the straight disabled guy who offered to help and had stayed in their life ever since. It would be rude not to show interest, so Iain asked the minimum number of questions. By the time she'd finished, it was getting late. The CD was over. Iain's libido was hardly diminished, but Meg had lost interest.

'I'm sorry,' she said when he tried to start up what the cramp had interrupted. 'It doesn't feel right. We've got all the time in the world, haven't we? You're a really good listener. I'd never have guessed that.'

The ride home felt much longer and colder than the one that had taken him there.

14

This was the first time that Jack had taken Harper out on a formal date on a Saturday night. His dad took him round there to collect her.

'Big place,' Dad commented. 'You could fit our house and garden on to their drive. I'll wait in the car, then.'

'Fine.' Jack was let in by Mr Simm, a small man with a grey moustache. He looked a good ten years older than Jack's father. Harper's father smiled but Jack could feel the hostility behind his handshake.

'Can I get you a drink before you go out, Jack?' Mrs Simm asked.

'No, thanks. My dad's waiting in the car.'

'I see.' At least Mrs Simm didn't ask him to invite Dad in. This was already awkward enough.

'About this party you're going to,' Mr Simm asked, as Jack began to wonder where Harper was. 'Whose house is it at?'

'I think the guy's name is Joe Clarke.'

'And the girl whose sixteenth it is lives with him?'

Jack began to guess where this was going. He wondered which would offend these uptight people more, that Meg was staying with a single, straight bloke or that her parents were lesbians.

'He's her godfather. She's staying there for a few weeks while her parents work abroad.'

The word *godfather* seemed to impress Mrs Simm, who managed half a smile. Mr Simm was not so easily placated. 'Work abroad, you say?'

'That's right,' Jack said.

'Doing what, exactly?'

Jack wasn't sure quite why he ought to defend Pat and Sarah, who he'd never really met, but a devilish impulse took him. 'They're missionaries,' he said.

'Missionaries?'

'Yeah. It's a very . . . religious family.' He looked at his watch. 'My dad . . .'

'Of course.' Mr Simm called upstairs. 'Harper, you're keeping this young man waiting.'

Instantly, he heard her coming down. She must have been waiting for the parental seal of approval.

'Nice to meet you,' Jack said, offering his hand and getting a longer handshake this time.

Mr Simm turned to his daughter. 'Don't forget what we said.'

In the driveway, Harper waggled her eyebrows. 'You passed the test!'

'You could have warned me. What was it he told you not to forget?'

'I promised not to get drunk and to book a taxi to get me home by twelve thirty. Sorry, I know it's a bit early.'

'No worries. Here's my dad. Dad, Harper.'

'You look like a million dollars, love. I hope Jack here's told you so.'

Dad was right. Jack cursed himself for saying nothing but Harper covered for him. 'Your son's the perfect gentleman. They don't make them like him where I come from.'

'And where would that be?' Dad asked, beginning an inquisition which would last the entire journey.

Joe was uncomfortable. 'Couldn't one of your friends do this?'

'They're not here yet. You are.'

When Meg bought the basque, at River Island, an assistant had helped her to put it on. Now, even as Meg expelled every breath in her body, Joe was having difficulty zipping it up at the back. This was his second attempt.

'Hang on.' As she jiggled about to get the right look, Joe looked away. Meg saw that the ribbons hung outside instead of in. Otherwise, it worked. She'd have to be very careful when dancing, though, or she'd flash the entire party.

'Now,' she said.

This time, Joe got it right. Meg hoped that Iain wouldn't have so much trouble unzipping it, later. 'What do you think?' she asked.

'It's very . . .' Joe stumbled for the right word. 'Fetching.'

He hurried back to the kitchen. Meg checked herself in the mirror. The black basque seemed to show everything off to its best advantage.

The doorbell rang. It was Iain, arriving early, as promised. They kissed.

'You look good enough to eat,' he said. 'Why don't we go to your room now and—'

She put a finger to his lips, shushing him. 'Later,' she whispered. 'The others will start arriving soon.'

Once, when Tom and Nina had the house to themselves, they would have rushed to the bedroom. Now they were more relaxed, taking a shower together first. As Tom soaped her back, Nina fell, banging her shoulder. She swore.

'How am I going to explain this bruise at school?'

Tom helped her up. 'Why should anybody at school see it?'

He found some Arnica to put on it. Then they towelled each other off and cuddled without hurrying to make love. Tom went to the loo. As he got back into bed, Nina dropped the bombshell.

'I've been thinking about going to college, doing 'A' levels.'

'What?'

'Then maybe going to university,' she continued. 'There's got to be more than staying round here all our lives.'

Tom felt floored. Was this about education, or travel, or about her leaving him?

'We can travel when we've saved some money,' he argued. 'Anyhow, who says there's anything wrong with living round here?'

'There's nothing wrong with it,' Nina said, pulling away from him. 'But I'm sixteen. I don't want the same things I wanted when I was fourteen.'

That was the thing, Tom thought. He'd fallen for a fourteen-year-old girl who looked and acted at least sixteen. Now that Nina was sixteen, she was changing on him. She wanted more.

'Are you trying to tell me something?' Tom asked. 'If you go to university, it'll be another five years before we can start a real life together. I love you, Neen, but I don't want to wait that long. I want to be with you.'

'I know. And I love you too. So we'll work it out, won't we?'

'I don't know,' Tom said, exasperated, watching his beautiful girlfriend get out of bed. Nina was the only woman he wanted. He'd near enough forgotten all the girlfriends he'd had before her. Yet, if she went to university, would he wait? And what about the two years between now and then? They could only afford a decent flat if Neen got a full-time job. Holding down two nights a week at the bakery while studying for GCSEs was hard enough. It would be impossible if she was doing 'A' levels. Had Nina already decided to dump him? If she had, maybe Tom would be better off finishing with her first.

'Are you going to get dressed?' Nina said, softly, as she brushed her hair in front of the mirror.

Tom pretended not to hear. He was in no hurry to go to this party, where all the other lads would be three or four years younger than him. He closed his eyes, affecting sleep. Then he felt Nina's hand, gently moving up his leg. Next, her moist lips, her tongue. Angry as Tom was with her, he couldn't resist. Bed would make everything all right. For now.

* * *

As they got out of the car, Jack told Harper how beautiful she looked.

'There's something I should warn you about,' he added. 'I told your dad Meg's parents are missionaries. Thought it was a better idea than telling the truth.'

'Which is what?'

'I have no idea what their jobs are, but they're a lesbian couple.'

Harper swore. 'That would have got him going. While we're at it, before you ring the bell, this Meg, how long did you go out with her for? Precisely.'

'We had one date. Hardly a date. A couple of kisses, that's all.'

'It's not going to be awkward?'

'Not at all,' Jack promised.

Meg answered the door. She had her hair pushed back and was wearing a black basque and a red, slit skirt. She looked sensational. For a moment, Jack envied whichever boy she ended up with tonight.

'I'd like you to meet Harper,' Jack said.

'It's a pleasure,' Meg said, in an unusually bubbly voice. 'How long have you two been together?'

'Jack and I got talking in the library a few days after I moved here,' Harper said. 'He's a fast mover.'

'In the library?' Meg said. 'I didn't know you were a reader, Jack.'

'I only go there to pick up women,' he said with a smile.

The house was smallish. In the living room, everything had been pushed against the walls to leave room to dance, but nobody was yet dancing.

'I brought a couple of dance mix tapes like you asked,' Jack said.

'Brilliant. Thank you.'

Jack looked around. The stereo system was very good. It must belong to Meg's godfather. His place didn't look like any house Jack had been in before. The living room was painted purple, while the kitchen was a bright, mediterranean green. There were posters and postcards all over the walls.

'Know everybody here?' Harper asked, as they chose what to drink.

'Yeah, most of them were at my old school.'

'Who's the guy with Meg? He looks familiar.'

Jack turned round. There, leaning over Meg, a lascivious grin on his face, was Iain. Jack hoped she had better taste than to end up with *him* tonight.

'That's Iain Foster. He goes to our college.'

'I think he's in my History class. So he's Meg's boyfriend?'

'Not as far as I know,' Jack replied.

'No? See where his hand is.'

Jack looked and realised that Harper was right. Iain's hand was inside Meg's short skirt, moving up her thigh as she talked with her mate Leah. As Jack watched, Meg smoothed her skirt. Instead of moving Iain's hand away, she stroked his wrist.

'I don't think you should do that kind of thing in public,' Harper said.

'You're right,' Jack said, 'but she seems to be enjoying it.'

They were sleeping together, he could tell, and it pissed him off. Iain could have anyone, so why had he picked the one girl who had turned Jack down? Iain must be the reason why Meg looked so radiant tonight. Cocky bastard.

'Who's that girl, watching them?' Harper wanted to know.

'I'll introduce you.'

It was Zoe Cumberland, who, uncharacteristically, was without a date. Jack didn't know what had happened to Iain and Zoe since the night of Todd's party. Presumably Iain had had his way with her then dumped her when he got bored, as per usual.

'Zoe, Harper.'

Side by side, the two girls were the same height.

Their luxuriant hair was the same length, halfway down their backs. It was a sight to see. Zoe, usually stand-offish, seemed to take to Harper. Jack's girlfriend told a joke and Zoe laughed far louder than the joke justified. Jack refilled his drink. He was joined by Iain.

'Who brought *her* here?' He was gesturing towards Harper.

'She's with me.'

'You're kidding.'

If Jack didn't know better, he'd say that Iain was jealous.

'What's she called?'

Jack gave him the basic details. 'I'll introduce you, if you like.'

'Not while she's with Zoe, thanks. I struck out there.'

'Oh. Right.' Jack was surprised by this admission of defeat, and suspicious. Maybe Iain was trying to tell him that it was safe to leave him around Harper. Which Jack didn't believe for a moment.

'How long have you been seeing Megan?' he asked.

'Since she came back from Australia,' Iain told him.

'She's looking good tonight.'

'So's yours.' Iain lowered his voice. 'Wanna swap?'

Beth was reluctant, but Leah persuaded her. 'You can't miss Meg's party. If I'm going on my own, so can you.

At least you don't have to face Iain Foster.'

Beth looked confused. 'Why should you be worried about seeing *him*?'

Leah fessed up. 'Remember that boy in Cornwall I told you about?'

When she was done, Beth's mood lightened a little. Everybody loved good gossip. In lowered voices, the two talked about sex. Beth went first.

'In a way, I wish I'd done it with somebody more experienced, like Iain.'

'It must be better to do it with somebody you care about,' Leah said. 'If it's his first time too, you're equals, aren't you? And he'd be more grateful.'

'We only did it the once,' Beth confessed. 'And Ross seemed more shocked than grateful. Doing it with him didn't make him go out with me.'

'I'm glad it's out of the way,' Leah said. 'I was becoming kind of obsessed with whether I'd be the last to do it. Now I feel . . . free. I'm in no hurry to go out with anyone. I just want to be me. If something happens, it happens.'

'*You* can say that,' Beth told her. 'You finished with him before he had the chance to finish with you. I feel free, too. Only I don't want to be free.'

They reached Meg's house. The door was ajar, so there was no need to ring the bell. Inside, loud music vibrated the framed film posters on the walls. People were beginning to dance. There were lots of couples, Leah saw, but no lads on their own. She looked around for Meg, or Nina, or Zoe. No sign.

More people arrived, including Tom and Nina. Leah could tell at once: something was wrong. Nina had been crying. Her make-up was wonky. Tom made a show of kissing both Beth and Leah on the cheek, but he looked angry.

'Where's the birthday girl?' he asked.

'No sign yet,' Beth said. 'We only just got here.'

'I expect she's down in her flat,' Leah guessed, 'holding private court.'

'Shall we go and see?' Nina suggested.

'Shall I check?' Leah said. 'Make sure she and Iain aren't up to anything?'

'Why don't you? Nothing down there you haven't seen before,' Beth quipped.

Leah gave her a stern look.

'What was that about?' Leah heard Nina ask as she went down the stairs. So her secret was out. She should have known better than to tell Beth. Meg could keep a secret. Zoe would have kept it a secret. So would Parvinder. But she, Beth and Nina were blabbermouths. They couldn't help it.

Leah was right. Meg was in the basement flat. So

were Zoe, Iain, Parvinder and Sanjeev, the five of them discussing the protocols surrounding a Sikh arranged marriage. Iain was at his most handsome, his short sideburns tightly trimmed. Sanjeev had a strong, almost fierce face, with dark, thick eyebrows and long hair.

'I'm not interrupting, am I?' Leah asked, breezing in. 'Only there are at least three of us waiting to give you a present. Happy birthday!'

Meg embraced her. 'Sorry. I was showing Parvinder the flat. She's not been before. Then we got carried away talking. I'll come up.'

'It's really noisy up there,' Leah said. 'I'll call the others down instead.' She whispered to Meg. 'I think Tom and Nina have had some kind of row.'

'Any idea what it's about?' Meg asked.

'None.' As the others came in, Leah glanced at Iain, who gave her a sheepish, almost benevolent smile. She smiled back, trying to be graceful but probably coming over as a grinning idiot. Introductions were made. Meg opened presents. Leah found herself next to Sanjeev, who told her about the course he was about to start at university. Tom and Nina stood in a corner, looking awkward. The six of them were chatting away when Joe appeared.

'Ah, there you are,' he said to Meg.

'I thought you were staying out of sight,' Meg teased him.

'I was, until a guy was sick right outside my study door.'

'A bit early for that,' Meg quipped. 'Sorry.'

'Somebody was sneaking shots of vodka chasers into his beer, or so he claimed. Anyway, after cleaning up, I thought I'd better make sure everything was OK. You've got about thirty people upstairs. The booze is running low and lots of people are looking for you.'

'I'll get up there,' Meg said. 'Sorry.'

'No need to worry. When you run out, there're forty cans of cheap lager at the back of the pantry. But once they're gone, that's your lot.'

'Thanks, Joe.' Megan led the way upstairs with Iain close behind. Leah saw the way that Joe looked at Iain. No love lost there. Tom pushed past her on the stairway, presumably in pursuit of Nina. Joe stayed behind. Leah looked back at him. If she had to choose a bloke to go out with, she wouldn't mind a younger version of Joe. He wasn't sexy or masculine but he was clever, caring, non-threatening. He was attractive, too, in an almost feminine way. She wondered why, in his mid-thirties, he was still single. Zoe joined her on the stairs.

'You look good tonight.'

'I wish I *felt* good,' Leah said. 'Parties always make me feel awkward.'

Zoe squeezed her shoulder. 'You don't show it, honest. I feel awkward at these things too.'

'*You* certainly don't show it,' Leah said. 'So don't say it. You're my role model.'

'I don't want to be anybody's role model,' Zoe told her. 'I want—'

Loud music drowned the rest of her words. They were back in the living room. Tom hurried out. It looked like he and Nina, having delivered their present, were making an early getaway. Iain Foster was dancing with Harper while her boyfriend, Jack, was talking to Joe in the hall. A guy who Leah didn't know, presumably a mate of Iain's, asked her if she fancied it. Leah said, 'Why not?' Somebody began passing round cans of weak but thirst-quenching lager. Leah took one, opened it without spilling any, then began to dance.

15

Tom and Nina were having a frantic, whispered conversation. Then Tom grabbed his coat and left. Nina remained at the far end of the hall, alone, hanging her head.

'Do you know her?' Joe asked Jack.

'Yeah. We used to go out.' A lifetime ago.

'Maybe you ought to have a word. If you like, when you're done, come up and have a look at the stuff I was telling you about. Top of the stairs on the right.'

'I will. Cheers.'

Tentatively, Jack joined Nina. 'Neen, are you all right?'

'What do you think?' Nina revealed red eyes and cheeks smeared with mascara. Jack held his arms out towards her. Nina, a full foot shorter than him, buried her head in his shoulder.

'Maybe I should have stuck with you,' she said, when she pulled away. 'Why do I always go for older guys who want more than I want to give?'

Jack didn't know what to say. Was she talking about sex? Or marriage? He had no idea. 'If Tom let you go, he's a fool,' Jack said.

'One of us must be a fool.' Nina managed a smile. 'Guess I look a mess.'

Jack handed her a tissue from his pocket. 'I think I need more than that,' Nina said, wiping away some of the tears. 'Do you know where the bathroom is?'

'Top of the stairs, but . . .' Jack pointed. There was a constant trail of people to the loo upstairs.

'I'll use the one in Meg's flat,' Nina said. 'You go back to Harper. Don't let Iain get too close to her,' she warned, before hurrying through the living room and down to the basement flat.

Harper, Jack saw, was talking to Zoe in the kitchen. Iain was in the corner of the living room, kissing Meg, his hand . . . no, Jack didn't want to look at that. Now was as good a time as any to go up to Joe's study.

He knocked before going in.

'Hey, Jack. I'll be with you in a minute.'

Jack looked around. In front of him was a huge drawing board, almost blocking out the window. Against the wall to his right were two computers, a G4 and one of the new iMacs, which Joe was working at. There were peripherals all over the place: a scanner, a zip drive, two printers and a mess of cable beneath the surfaces. One of the remaining walls was covered in shelves from floor to ceiling, housing a very serious comics collection. The other was covered in framed artwork, some by artists that Jack recognised, like the Hernandez brothers, who did *Love And Rockets*. There was also a photograph. It showed Joe with his arm round Megan, aged ten or so. Two grinning women (presumably her mothers) stood beside them. Sydney Opera House was in the background.

'What are you working on?' Jack asked the cartoonist. On the screen was an image of a pretty girl driving a futuristic car.

'I'm collaborating with this guy Dave in San Francisco on a short series for Fantagraphics. We call it *TroubleGum*. It's *The Archies* for the new century, teens of the future, that kind of thing.'

'What's *The Archies*?' Jack asked, and Joe was off, explaining his comic and how it fitted in with stuff from the past. As he opened the draft pages, Jack couldn't help but notice how the lead character looked like Megan, while her friends resembled younger versions of the three adults on the photo behind them.

Bethany felt left out. Nobody had asked her to dance and even if they did, a dance was all they would get. She was still fed up about Ross. Normally, she'd start dancing on her own, or with Leah. But all evening she'd been distracted, watching Jack Green and his girlfriend, Ross's sister. Harper was a real looker. Iain Foster had begun dancing alongside her. Meg ought to watch him. When Jack returned to the room, Harper gave him a small wave, but continued dancing next to Iain. Jack went to get a fresh drink in the kitchen.

Now might be the time. Harper and Ross were only a school year apart. It was possible, probable even, that Ross talked to her. Bethany only had to ask. Was Ross always this unreasonable when it came to relationships? She joined Jack.

'Having a good time?'

'Yes. I've been talking to Joe about comics. You should see some of the—'

Beth interrupted. 'Jack, can you help me with something?'

'Um, sure.'

'I wanted a word with Harper. About Ross.'

'Her brother? Nice kid. He slaughtered me at table tennis last month.'

'He's hardly a kid,' Beth said, not sure why she was defending the lad who was refusing to go out with her.

Jack shrugged. 'I guess not. Year Nine, isn't he? Harper said how he used to go to your church's under-fourteen discos.'

'Year Nine.' Bethany repeated the words mechanically, not sure she was taking in what Jack was saying. Ross couldn't be two school years below her, could he?

'You help run those discos, don't you? I suppose that's how you know him? Harper was saying how he'd stopped this term because he was getting too old . . . Beth? You all right?'

Beth realised that Jack had put an arm beneath her elbow to support her.

'I'm sorry,' she said. 'I started feeling a little faint. Must be the drink, and the heat.'

'It *is* hot in here,' Jack said, as Harper stopped dancing and joined them. Jack handed her a drink. Somehow, Beth got herself together and spoke to Harper.

'I was wondering why your Ross had stopped coming to the discos that I help run. But Jack tells me he's gotten too old.'

'That's right,' Harper said. 'He'll be fourteen in a couple of weeks. Know of any church discos for fourteens and over?'

'Why a church disco?' Beth asked.

'Harper's family are religious,' Jack said, half serious. 'They wouldn't want Ross meeting loose women who might lead him astray.'

'Are you all right?' Harper asked Bethany. 'Your face is really flushed.'

'I-I think I ought to go outside for a while, cool down,' she stuttered.

'Want us to come with you?' Jack offered.

'No, I'll be fine, honest.' Bethany opened the kitchen door and hurried down the steps, into the mild night. It was a long, thin garden. A few feet away from her, she could hear a couple doing something they'd probably rather keep private. Beth walked rapidly past them, towards the far end of the lawn which backed on to the park. How could she not have realised that Ross was so young? It made sense of everything. She had never asked him his age. She had only assumed. He wasn't at the disco to help, like her. He was taking his first steps at hanging out with the opposite sex. She, being older, had taken advantage of him. Beth felt incredibly humiliated. And her humiliation would be a thousand times worse when the others found out. Did they have to find out?

Not far from her, somebody was talking. Bethany couldn't make out the words, but she could make out the voice: Nina. She sounded upset. Beth started to go over, then heard a new voice, one which wasn't Tom's. The moon came out from behind a cloud. Bethany saw why Nina was such a long way from the house. The guy she was with was holding her. In silhouette it was hard to tell, but it looked like they were kissing.

It was all too much to take in. Beth decided to forget what she'd seen. She would go back inside and check whether Leah was ready to leave.

16

The living room smelt of cheap beer, sweat and cigarettes. Zoe retreated to the hall, where she waited for her taxi. She looked around for Nina. Her flat was on Zoe's way home, so it made sense for them to travel together. Nina's boyfriend, Tom, was long gone but Nina hadn't left with him.

Had she got off with someone else? It wouldn't surprise Zoe. Nina had been pretty promiscuous before Tom came along. Through the doorway, Zoe watched Leah slow-dancing with one of Iain's smarmy mates. He had his tongue in her ear, a sight which offended Zoe. There was no accounting for taste.

Meg and Iain were also having a close dance, patently hoping that everybody would soon leave them alone so that they could do horizontally what they were practising standing up. Parvinder and Sanjeev seemed to have slipped away. Jack and Harper had left at twenty past twelve. Zoe guessed that Harper had some kind of curfew, though she hadn't said anything about it. They'd had a long chat earlier. Harper was nice, but slightly odd, Zoe thought. She wondered if Jack knew about all of her views. He'd made some joke about religion when they first got talking. But Harper seemed deadly serious in her beliefs. Sometimes Zoe wished that her own convictions were so clear cut.

Leah appeared, looking angry about something. 'We're leaving.'

'Are you all right?' Zoe asked.

'I've been fending off Roger Twelve Hands, one of Iain's mates. When I told him where to get off, know what he said? *Iain told me you were up for it.*'

'Nice,' Zoe said. 'So Iain was the guy in Cornwall, was he?'

'Umm . . . I was going to tell you.'

'She really was,' Bethany said, following Leah into the hall. 'She only told *me* tonight.'

Both Parvinder and Zoe had sussed it weeks back. Leah's story about the bloke in Cornwall was a fairy tale. All the same, Zoe had been surprised that Leah had succumbed to Iain. She was even more surprised that Iain had picked her. Was *any* girl not his type? At this rate, he was going to work his way through all of Zoe's friends. Was it some kind of revenge against Zoe for the night of Todd's party?

A horn sounded outside.

'Come on, we can all get in my taxi,' she told the others.

'It's only a ten minute walk,' Beth said.

'But it's on the way,' Zoe insisted. 'You might as well keep me company. Neither of you have seen Nina, have you?'

'I think she left ages ago,' Leah said.

'I guess she must have,' Zoe agreed. 'Let's go.'

At last, it looked like everyone had left. Zoe and her mates had gone off in a taxi and there was no sign of Joe. Probably in bed. Meg was emptying ash-trays, opening windows. Iain did his bit by sweeping up the crisps and French bread that some slobs had trodden into the carpet. Then he caught Meg by the arm.

'Let's leave the rest till morning, shall we?'

'Easy for you to say. You won't be here.'

'I will,' Iain said. 'I told my mum I was staying the night at a mate's.'

'That's sweet.' Meg put one arm around his waist, then, with her free hand caressed his cheek and gave him an enormous wet kiss.

'Let's go downstairs,' Iain whispered, when they broke apart.

'What for?' Meg teased, a hand inside his shirt.

'You're right,' Iain said. 'Let's do it right here.'

He pulled her on to the sofa. He had been waiting for this moment all night, all month in fact. Tonight, with Meg so alluring and Harper on Jack's arm, looking so, so tasty, and, finally, gorgeous, oh-so-sure-of-herself Zoe, reminding him of what he'd missed, tonight, Iain had never been more up for it.

'Iain, what are you doing? Don't be so rough.'

'Relax,' Iain said, trying to undo her tight, black basque.

'Iain, stop. I'm not ready . . .'

Iain pulled back for a moment, not believing what he was hearing. Meg seemed to relax. 'Wow,' she said. 'You don't like to waste time, do you?'

Iain stroked her hair, then slid his hand inside her skirt, slipping down her knickers so that they were halfway off her bottom. 'If you're not ready now,' he told her, 'you never will be.'

He thought she was going along with it.

'Iain, I'm knackered,' she said.

'This'll wake you up,' he promised.

He was just sliding off his jeans when the door opened.

'Sorry,' Nina said. 'Are we interrupting something?'

Meg squirmed away from under Iain and pulled her knickers up. As she did, Joe walked in. 'Everything all right?' he asked.

Iain grunted. Where the hell had these two come from? Why hadn't he carried Meg down to the basement, where nobody would have interrupted them?

'Iain was just leaving,' Meg said, in a surprisingly firm voice.

Glaring at the intruders, Iain zipped up his jeans and looked around for his shirt. There was an anxious silence, which was broken by Joe.

'Anybody want coffee?' he asked.

Iain recovered himself enough to kiss Meg on the cheek. 'I'll call tomorrow, OK?'

She didn't reply. Iain got out of the house at the speed of light, wishing he'd brought his bike. It was a four mile walk home.

'You OK?' Nina asked. Joe had left her and Meg alone.

'Yeah. Think so. Iain's a bit . . . full on.'

'He's a horny sixteen-year-old lad. What do you expect?'

Meg shrugged. 'More than a fumbled grope for foreplay.'

'You two still haven't done it yet?' Nina sounded amazed.

'I've only been going out with him for four weeks!'

'Lots of boys won't wait that long,' Nina told her.

'Well they'll have to if they want to get anywhere with me.'

'And, if you don't mind me saying . . . to Iain, that top must look a lot like an invitation.'

'You sound like my gran!' Meg complained. But she *had* meant to sleep with Iain tonight. Why had he ruined it?

'I thought you wanted to do it.'

'I thought I wanted to, too. But it has to be right. I have to feel right.'

'You're not waiting for a love job, are you?' Nina asked. 'Because you must know that Iain's not like that.'

'I know. But I thought he'd be different with me.'

'How much do you like him?' Nina asked, gently.

'I'm a little in love, a lot in lust, I think. Only, the lust isn't there when he's drunk and just wants someone to relieve his hard-on.'

'I see.' Nina sat on the edge of the sofa, her profile stark in the red light which Joe had set up for the dance floor. She looked much older than Meg felt.

'What happened with you and Tom?' Meg asked, wanting to change the subject.

'I think we broke up,' she said. 'I was at the bottom of the garden for ages. Joe found me. He was really helpful, talking everything through. He told me about this girl he was once in love with.'

Meg was about to ask about this when Joe poked his head round the door.

'Your taxi's here,' he told Nina. 'Do you have enough money?'

'Yes, thanks.' Nina turned to Meg. 'Wish I had a godfather like him.'

'He's one of a kind.'

'Thank him for looking after me.'

'I will. See you Monday.'

In the kitchen, Joe had put on some bluesy piano music. Wordlessly, Meg helped him clear up.

'Go to bed if you want,' Joe said, as he washed glasses. 'I'll finish in here. You know me, I won't be in bed for an hour yet.'

'I'm not tired now,' Meg said. The encounter with Iain had woken her up. 'Nina says thanks for talking to her, by the way. She said you were really helpful.'

'I found her crying in the garden,' Joe said. 'She's a nice girl.'

'She said you talked about a woman you were in love with.'

'That'd be Christine,' he said. 'She was in the year below me at school.'

'You went out with her?'

Joe nodded. 'First love of my life. Only love, really.'

'Then you went to university.'

'That's right. Where I met Pat and Sarah.'

Hearing him speak of her parents, Meg felt a crushing awareness of how much she missed them both. Her eyes watered.

'You OK?'

'Sorry,' Meg said, tiring. 'I think maybe I'm starting to crash.'

'Not surprised. It's nearly two. I'll tell you the rest another day. Unless. . .'

'Unless what?' Meg asked.

'I promised Pat and Sarah I'd look out for you, but
. . .'

'But what?'

Joe was more than a little embarrassed. 'It's none of my business what you get up to with Iain. It doesn't matter whether I like him or not. As long as you know what you're doing.'

'I . . .' Meg tried to say that she did know what she was doing, but that would be a lie. 'He's had a lot of girlfriends. He expects things to happen quickly.'

'I thought it might be something like that.'

'I can handle him.'

'Are you sure?' Joe asked, gently. 'Only, when Nina and me walked in, you didn't *look* like you were handling him. To be honest, you looked scared.'

Meg was silent. Joe put his arm around her.

'Not exactly scared,' she said, in a quiet voice. 'Overwhelmed, maybe.' She hesitated, holding back tears. 'What's wrong with me?'

'Nothing,' Joe said, putting an arm around her. 'There's nothing at all wrong with you. Do me a favour. Don't try to do all your growing up at once. There's no hurry. The world will wait for you. Once your childhood's gone, it's gone.'

Meg cried into his smoky shirt. Tonight, childhood seemed a long way away.

17

Most weeks Bethany didn't go to a Sunday service. Living at home was like going to church every day. But the week after Meg's party, she arrived at nine twenty-two, slipping unnoticed into a pew otherwise occupied by OAPs. Her mother's church was the one place she could be sure to see Ross.

Bethany didn't want to go out with Ross. Not any more. What she wanted to know, for her own peace of mind, was when he had found out how old she was.

Ross arrived with his parents at nine twenty-eight, as usual. (Harper always went to the evening service on her own.) Beth had observed this last week, the day after the party. Then, she'd been upset, and couldn't think of a way to separate Ross from his parents. Today she was determined.

Mum's sermon was about hypocrisy, the little things people say and do which they don't think of as dishonest. If you wanted to be a good person, where did you draw the line? Not telling someone a dress didn't suit them? Always buying Fair Trade coffee or free-range eggs? Stealing stationery from the office? Fiddling expenses? Only breaking your marriage vows when you're out of town?

Beth knew the arguments already. Mum and Dad discussed stuff like this at the dinner table, always trying to involve her, their only child. Maybe they only had those discussions because of her. Beth could work out the 'right' answers with the same part of her brain she used for multiple choice tests. She knew the basic principles. You had to try and be good all the time. We all slipped up, but if you made conscious compromises, you were on a slippery slope. When you sinned, you had to beg forgiveness. But all that was her parents' code, not hers. Beth didn't know what her code was, not yet. She didn't know what principles applied to having sex with Ross Simm.

Outside, after the service, Mr Simm chatted to Mum while his wife looked on, admiringly. Beth took a deep breath, then walked straight over to the four of them. Ross didn't see her coming. But Mum did.

'Do you know my daughter, Bethany . . . ?'

As the three Simms turned, Beth planted a hand firmly on Ross's shoulder.

'Do you mind if I borrow Ross for five minutes? It's about helping with this term's discos . . .'

She steered Ross to the weeping willow on the edge of the graveyard. Then she gave him his cover story.

'If your parents ask what I wanted, I tried to persuade you to help with the under-fourteen discos. You said 'no' because you'd feel uncomfortable, only being a few months older than the oldest kids there. OK?'

His face went red.

'When did you find out?' Ross asked, looking away from her.

'From your sister and her boyfriend, last Saturday night. When did *you* find out?'

Ross replied in a shuffling, muted monologue. 'I sort of suspected. Then, when you said how your mate used to go out with Jack . . . well, I knew he'd just finished Year Eleven. So I guessed you must be a year or two older than me.'

'Do I *look* like I'm in Year Nine?' Beth asked, angrily.

'Some of the girls in my year, it's really hard to tell . . . I thought you were at the disco because you were thirteen, like me.'

'All right, all right.' Beth knew she looked young for her age. It was probably the main reason she'd never had a boyfriend.

'You could at least have told me,' she said.

'I was embarrassed.'

'I'll bet you told your mates that we did it.'

'I didn't tell anyone,' Ross said, beginning to blush. 'Anyway, we didn't actually do it, did we?'

'What do you mean?'

'I didn't manage to . . .' Ross, face becoming pinker, hesitated, 'put it in.'

'But you . . .' Bethany didn't know how to talk about this. 'You're sure?'

'I'm sure. I've got to go.'

Beth glanced round the tree. The Simms were standing by the churchyard gate, looking in her direction.

'Yes,' she said. 'You'd better go. Forget what happened. Nobody knows about it except us and we'll pretend that nothing went on. Deal?'

'Deal.'

He scurried away. Beth began to feel bad about what they'd done. Only, how could she be the bad person, when she was as innocent as he was? Who was she kidding? Innocence had nothing to do with it. She'd been so anxious to catch up with her friends that she'd practically seduced a boy who wasn't ready for sex. She was an embarrassment, to herself and to others. And they hadn't even done it right. That was the biggest embarrassment of all.

* * *

Meg had been ducking Iain's calls for a week. It was easy. All she had to do was keep her mobile switched off. Iain didn't like to call her on the land line (Joe always picked up first, in case it was work). The messages he left were increasingly tetchy. She'd texted him a couple of times, saying she'd catch up with him at the weekend. But she and Zoe had been to a concert on Saturday night. Now it was Sunday evening and she still hadn't phoned.

If you're going to dump him, dump him was Zoe's advice. *Don't let him have the pleasure of chucking you.* But Meg was dithering. There were a lot of good things about Iain and only a few bad things. Admittedly, they were big bad things. She'd tried to ignore the nastier stories. You had to take people as you found them, not rely on gossip, most of which came from girls he'd either chucked or never asked out in the first place. But Meg did believe Zoe and Leah. Sex was the main thing on Iain's mind. Once Meg succumbed, they were unlikely to last long as a couple.

What was wrong with that? Forget love. Meg wanted to be experienced. She wanted to be able to join in explicit conversations. She wanted not to feel like a hypocrite when she gave a knowing laugh in response to a gag she hadn't really understood. She wanted, like Leah, to have got it over with, so that she could concentrate on more important things. It was Sunday evening. Meg could go there now. Iain's last message said that he'd be in, baby-sitting his younger sister. Meg could call a taxi, give him a nice surprise. Then Zoe and Parvinder could fight it out over which of them would be the last to go. *Yes*, Meg thought. *Why not*?

Her taxi got her there at a quarter past eight. There was only one car in the big drive, which meant that Iain's parents had already gone out. Meg had been to the house once before, on an afternoon when she'd skived off school (she hated Games). It was an impressive place, bigger than Zoe's, with six bedrooms, twice as many as the Fosters actually needed. Iain had wanted to do it that afternoon, but, uncomfortable with the situation, she'd made him settle for less.

She should have rung first.

Iain might have headphones on, or not be answering the door because he wasn't expecting a caller. People rarely visited without calling first. Meg rang the bell a second time. She heard footsteps.

'Who is it?' A girl's voice. Meg tried to remember the younger sister's name. Janice. No, Janine.

'Janine? Hi. It's Meg, Iain's friend.'

Janine opened the door on the chain. 'He's not in. Dunno where he is.'

'But he told me . . . would you mind if I came in? I'll ring his mobile.'

'I guess.' The girl undid the chain. Meg followed her into the huge house. Janine was already Meg's height and a little gawky. Her long, dark hair was tied back and her figure was carefully concealed by a navy blue tracksuit. Once she lost the pink pimples that blemished her face, she would probably be very pretty.

'You're in on your own?' Meg asked.

'Iain's meant to be baby-sitting. But I don't need a baby-sitter and he's been in a strop since last weekend. Something to do with you?'

'Probably,' Meg admitted.

'Good for you. He's so arrogant. He thinks he's God's gift.'

'He's very popular,' Meg said. 'I don't suppose he can help it.'

'Girls always make excuses for him. They want to think he's wonderful so they can justify throwing themselves at his feet.'

'Whereas to you, he's your bossy, irritating older brother,' Meg suggested.

'Something like that. Go ahead, ring him.'

Meg did. An automated voice answered.

'I'll text him in a minute,' she said.

'I know about you,' Janine told her. 'Everyone says you're a lesbian.'

Meg was taken aback. 'People say that in *Year Eight*?'

'No, I heard it in Year Seven. Is that why you're going out with Iain? Do you want him to convert you? It must be rubbish, being a lesbian.'

'I'm not . . .' Megan stopped herself from denying her parents' sexual preference. She'd thought she'd got past all the gossip by the beginning of Year Ten, when she'd had her first boyfriend. For four years, though, from the last year of primary school to the third year of secondary, the teasing was constant. She had learnt to hate the teasers, to ridicule them, to be sorry for them and, at the same time, to fear them. She had also learnt never to explain. 'My mum's a lesbian,' she said. 'Doesn't mean I am.'

'You've got two mums.' Janine sounded curious, not insulting.

'That's right.'

'And you live with the bloke who's your real father?'

'Who told you that?'

'Iain.'

Meg put her head in her hands. What on earth had she told Iain for? Even her friends didn't know about Joe, though one or two had sort of guessed.

'He shouldn't have told you that. Who else knows?'

'I haven't told anyone. Dunno about Iain.'

'Can you do me a favour, Janine?'

'Jan. What is it?'

'Don't tell anyone about that. It's a secret.'

'Why?'

'Because . . . because Joe and me still have things to work out. I'm living with him because my parents are working away for a term.'

'Selfish parents you've got. Maybe you're better off with him.'

Meg tried to laugh. 'That's a pretty negative attitude you have.'

Janine shrugged dismissively. 'I think that's Iain,' she said.

Meg heard movement in the hall. 'I enjoyed talking to you,' she told Jan.

'I'll keep your secret,' Jan replied.

The door opened. Meg heard Iain's voice. 'Jan? You got company?'

'No. You have.'

Meg turned to Iain with a conciliatory smile. Then she saw that he wasn't alone.

'Hello, Taz,' she said.

The older girl was wearing blue jeans and a tight, navy blue tank top. She had the grace to look embarrassed. Iain, however, took the situation in his stride.

'Meg, you should have told me you were coming. I bumped into Taz at the chippy. We were . . .' He hesitated, seeing the scepticism in Meg's eyes. Then he turned to Taz. 'Could you give us a couple of minutes?'

Taz looked faintly amused. 'Sure.'

Iain led Meg into the kitchen. 'It's not what you think. We're just—'

'After a repeat performance of what happened at Todd Smith's party?'

'Oh. You know about that.'

'This is a small town,' Megan told him. 'It's hard to keep secrets. But I've never told anyone but you that Joe's my biological father. Who have you told?'

'No one. I swear.'

Meg gave him a long, hard stare. Iain seemed to twig.

'I'll kill her,' Iain said. 'She's been reading my diary again.'

'You keep a *diary*? I'd have thought a little black book was more your style.'

'I guess I deserve that,' Iain said.

'I guess you do. Now call me a taxi, please.'

Iain softened his voice. 'Meg, don't be like this. It's only—'

'Ask them to make it quick.'

Iain did as he was told. Then, ham-fistedly, he began to explain. 'You don't know what it's like, being a lad. It aches. It stands to attention at the slightest provocation.'

'Did nobody ever teach you to jerk-off?' Meg asked, caustically.

Iain ignored this comment, as though it were beneath him. 'Me and Taz, it's casual. She knows what I'm like. I couldn't wait any longer, that was all. Give me another chance.'

'I don't think so,' Meg told him. 'I think I'd feel cheap and I can live without that. Just do me a favour, don't tell the world about Joe.'

Taz knocked on the door. 'There's a taxi outside,' she said.

'Perfect timing,' Meg said, picking up her bag. 'He's all yours.'

18

Jack had never had a girlfriend in his room before. The Greens lived in a two-bedroomed terrace. Until this week, when Mark, his elder brother, started university, Jack had had to share a room. Today Mum and Dad were driving Mark to Hope University. Then they were staying overnight in Liverpool. For the first evening ever, Jack had the house to himself.

When Harper was round before, Jack hadn't known what kind of place she was used to. Orwell Road wasn't some leafy, wide street with burglar alarms and big drives, like hers. Jack meant to do better for himself than an end terrace. But he wasn't ashamed of this house, or his room. He wasn't going to defend it to her.

He needn't have worried. There was nothing snobbish about Harper. All she said, after he'd made them a drink, was: 'Let's see your famous room, then.'

He took her up to the room, a back bedroom facing on to the yard.

'It must be strange,' she said, 'being on your own after all these years.'

'I've been looking forward to it.'

'You're bound to miss your brother.'

'Mark and I used to fight all the time,' Jack told her. 'Up until he was about fifteen. This room was never big enough for the both of us.'

Harper laughed. 'What are you going to do with it, now that he's gone?'

Jack looked around. 'Got to keep the second bed. He'll still be home for the holidays. And students get loads of holidays. But we could push them together . . .'

Harper chuckled. 'I'm going to get you a poster for that big, empty space,' she said, pointing at where Mark's Angelina Jolie pin-up used to be. 'What was there before?'

'You don't want to know,' Jack said. 'Why don't you come and sit here?'

She joined him on the bed and they kissed. She was the best kisser. Her tongue was soft and moist, moving slowly around his. They held each other firmly, not tightly, her fingers stroking his neck sexily, moving inside his T-shirt, along his back. As if by instinct, they readjusted the way they were sitting so that he could reach inside her woollen sweater. After a few minutes, he managed to undo her bra. A little while later, they were further on than they had been in her bedroom, three weeks before. They were one step away from being naked. But, when he tried to take the next step, she stopped him.

'That's as far as we go.'

Ten minutes later, when he tried again, she said, 'I meant it.'

'It's OK,' Jack said, though it wasn't, not really. 'I can be patient.'

'You'll have to be a lot more than patient,' Harper said, softly but firmly.

Jack asked her what she meant.

'What's wrong?' Joe asked Meg. 'Wasn't he there?'

'He was there all right,' Meg said. She'd hoped to avoid Joe, but he'd heard her come in. 'So was Taz Newton.'

Joe was confused. 'I take it Taz is a girl?'

'He said there was nothing in it, but I know he's been with her before. She wasn't there to help him with his homework.'

'Maybe there's another, innocent, explanation,' Joe suggested.

'No, he more or less admitted it. He said that, since I wasn't sleeping with him, he had to find someone else who would, that it had been too long since he'd had sex. Is that right? Is that how it works for men?'

'Not exactly. But there are . . . other releases, without being unfaithful.'

Meg knew what he meant. Everybody masturbated, Sarah had told her once. Even people in couples. So must Iain, even if he wouldn't admit as much to her.

'How do you feel about Iain?' Joe asked. 'Are you in love with him?'

Meg shook her head. 'I fancy him like mad. I hoped we'd fall in love. But, if I'm honest, it's more that I want everyone to see I'm going out with him. He's a challenge, I guess. I want to know if I can tame him. Looks like I failed.'

'There are always guys like Iain around. They have a lot of sex, but I suspect they don't have very fulfilling relationships.'

'You're just saying that to comfort me,' Meg muttered.

'Comfort myself, more like. Want a drink?' Joe reached for the wine rack. 'You don't feel you have something to prove, do you?'

'How do you mean?'

'*My parents might be gay but I'm straight*, that kind of thing.'

'If I'd needed to prove that, I could have lost my virginity a year ago,' Meg said. 'But I'd have been letting myself down, wouldn't I?'

Joe, busy opening the wine, didn't reply. They drifted into silence.

'You started to tell me something last week, after the party,' Meg said, a few minutes later. 'About a girl called Christine. Who was she?'

'She was the love of my life,' Joe said, softly.

'What happened to her?'

Joe took a big slurp of wine. 'She died,' he said.

'Oh God, I'm sorry. I didn't know. I thought . . .'

'You got the impression that she left me and broke my heart,' Joe filled in for her. 'Which is exactly what she did. We were in a car together when it happened. She was driving. A lorry came round a blind bend way too fast and . . .'

'That's how you damaged your leg.'

'Yeah. I woke up two days later in hospital. I didn't give a damn about my leg. All I wanted to know about was Christine. The doctors and nurses wouldn't say. Then my mum came and broke it to me as gently as she could.'

'How old were you?'

'I was eighteen. She was seventeen. She'd passed her driving test three weeks before. I'd been seeing her for a couple of months. We were very close – good mates, but really in love, too. She was gorgeous.'

'She was your first . . . ?'

Joe shook his head. 'We talked about making love. She wanted to wait until the moment was absolutely right, special. And I was fine with that.'

'You never . . .'

'We were on our way to go camping in the Lake District. Maybe it would have happened then.'

'That's so dreadful,' Meg said. 'How did you cope?'

'I didn't, really. I nearly gave up my university place, but my parents prodded and pushed me, so I went. I was on crutches for the whole of the first year. The only close friend I made was Pat. Then she met Sarah while she was backpacking in the holidays. I thought I'd lost her, too. Later, though, they asked me . . . Yeah, well . . . you know the rest of the story.'

'That was a big thing to ask somebody who was only twenty-one.'

'It was. But you make big decisions when you're young because you think you know it all, that you're ready for whatever the world's going to throw at you. Whereas, at that age, you're still a kid, basically.'

'What does that make me?' Meg asked.

'I don't know,' her father said. 'But I'll tell you

something, looking at you now: you're the best decision I ever made.'

'Until you're *married*?' Jack couldn't believe what he was hearing. 'Nobody thinks like that any more, do they?'

'I do,' Harper said. 'Don't make me feel bad about it.'

'Is it your religion?'

'Yes, it is my religion. But I'm not a crank. Every religion is against sex before marriage.'

'And I'll bet every religion is ignored, too,' Jack argued. 'That's so out of date.'

'I'm trying to be a good person. I care about you. If you care about me, you won't try to make me do something I don't want to do.'

'Of course not. Only . . .' Jack realised that there was no answer to her last argument. 'At least allow me the possibility that you might change your mind.'

Harper didn't answer directly. 'I'm not saying we can't talk about it. Out of interest, how many girls have you done it with?'

Jack hesitated. Girls weren't meant to ask questions like that. But he couldn't lie. 'None,' he admitted. 'A couple of times, I've come close to . . . you know.'

'Like us just now?' Jack nodded. 'Who with?' Harper

asked, her voice curious, almost amused. 'Meg?'

'No, a girl called Nina. She was up for it but I guess I wasn't confident enough. Then there was this girl at a party. That meant nothing.'

Nearly naked in each other's arms, they talked about who they'd been out with. Harper had had a couple of serious boyfriends. One of them dumped her when she wouldn't sleep with him, the other had never even tried it on. She'd been keen on them both, she said. 'But I'm keener on you. I really feel close to you.'

'Me too.'

'Then isn't this enough?' she asked, nibbling his ear.

'For now,' he said, hiding his frustration. 'For now.'

'One thing I find hard to understand,' Meg said to Joe. 'Christine – that was half your lifetime ago, your whole adult life. Why have you stayed single?'

'Because I never met anyone who came close.'

'But you must have had girlfriends.'

'Not really. I was on anti-depressants for most of my twenties. Now and then Pat and Sarah would try and set me up with someone, but most of their social circle is gay. By the time my career got going, I was too set in my ways for many women to be interested. I mean, look at me. I'm hardly the world's greatest catch.'

'Rubbish. There's nothing wrong with you that some

decent clothes and a good haircut wouldn't fix.'

Joe laughed. 'Maybe you're right. I'm seeing someone this week, as it happens. First time in a couple of years. So maybe there's life in the old dog yet.'

The phone rang. It would be the twice weekly call from Australia, where it was early tomorrow morning. 'Better answer that,' Meg said, going into the hall.

Her parents said the work was going well. Meg insisted that she was working hard, too, which was nearly the truth. At least she wasn't behind. When Pat asked her about boyfriends, she was cagey. 'Nothing serious,' she insisted.

'And how are you and Joe getting on?'

'Great.' Or they would be, now that she'd finished with Iain. 'He was just telling me about Christine, and the accident.'

'Poor Joe. He's never got over that. Sometimes I wonder if he ever will.'

'He's seeing someone this week.'

'Really? Do you know who?' Pat asked.

'Afraid not.'

'She'll have to be understanding, is all I can say. We've tried to set Joe up so many times, but he can be very flaky.'

'When it comes down to it,' Meg said, 'he's shy. That's all.'

Sarah had a proposal: Christmas in Sydney. 'Joe, too. How about it?'

'Sounds brilliant. Turkey on the beach. Then do we all fly back together?'

'That's the plan. You're sure there's no boyfriend you'll be deserting?'

'I'm concentrating all my energy on my GCSEs,' Meg promised, and she meant it. Work was what she was going to do. Boyfriends could wait.

19

'This is an historic evening,' Leah announced outside the cinema on Saturday evening. 'For the first time since the start of Year Nine, we're all single.'

Parvinder coughed.

'Or practically married,' Leah corrected herself.

'You never know,' Nina said. 'Zoe might turn up having met Mr Right.'

'Zoe's a perfectionist,' Leah told the others. 'If she ever finds Mr No Faults, I'll guarantee you one thing: he'll be boring as hell.'

'So which film are we going to see?' Meg asked.

'We can't decide without Zoe,' Bethany argued. 'We're bound to choose something too "lowbrow" or "mindlessly violent".'

'Screw that,' Leah argued. 'I want to see the new James Bond.'

'Me too,' Zoe said. The five turned to face Zoe, who'd been listening to their conversation unnoticed. Leah gasped. Parvinder smiled enigmatically. Nina wore an embarrassed grin. Bethany's jaw dropped and Meg looked nonplussed. On the whole, Zoe was pleased with the reaction.

'I like it,' Leah said, gratifyingly. 'You're really *you*.'

'What's with the glasses?' Nina asked. 'I didn't know you wore glasses.'

'I've had contacts since Year Seven,' Zoe said. 'But glasses are much more convenient and I wanted a new look.'

'But your beautiful hair!' Meg said.

'I like it short,' Zoe told her. 'If I change my mind, I can always grow it back.'

'Yeah, if you've got a spare year or two,' Megan murmured.

Nobody commented on her clothes. Zoe had ditched her normal short skirt and little top for a plain t-shirt and jeans. She decided to bring the subject up herself.

'What do you think of the new look?' she asked the others.

'You don't *want* a boyfriend, do you?' Nina said.

'That's right,' Zoe said. 'I don't want a bloke who's interested in my breasts, or my legs or the fact that in the right light I look like some model or actress. I'm fed up of being leered at by strangers. So I asked myself – what can I do about it? And the answer was: dress the way you feel.'

'Congratulations,' Parvinder said. 'You've shocked us all. Now, I suppose you want to see some film with subtitles to go with your new image.'

'No,' Zoe said. 'James Bond it is.'

'We've been going out for three months,' Jack reminded Harper.

'Two and a half,' she corrected him.

'It's not like this is some casual thing. I care about you.'

'I care about you, too.' She kissed him. 'It's got nothing to do with that.'

Harper had had this discussion before. Her second serious boyfriend, Paul, had been three years older than her. He'd acted like he was bestowing a huge favour on Harper, going out with a fifteen-year-old girl. The least she could do to repay his generosity was to have sex with him. When Harper kept turning him down, he'd finished with her, but not before suggesting that she must be a lesbian.

Harper knew she wasn't gay. She enjoyed the cuddling, the caressing, the long kisses Jack gave her. But she didn't feel frustrated that they couldn't go all the way. Friends at her old school had slept with their boyfriends and told her about it. Often they ended up complaining. It was all over in minutes, they said. Or seconds. The lads were only interested in their own pleasure. There was no foreplay, no kissing or cuddling afterwards. Pretty soon, they took the sex for granted, and couldn't wait to get their clothes back on once they were finished.

'Does it bother you that I don't believe in God?' Jack asked.

'Not really,' Harper replied, though it did bother her a little. Harper wasn't as religious as her parents. She didn't think sex before marriage was a sin. But she wouldn't feel right, doing it with someone she didn't plan to spend the rest of her life with. And, face it, at sixteen, you weren't choosing a husband. The decider was this: when she had children, in ten or fifteen years' time, she wanted to be able to tell her daughter that her father was the only man she'd ever been with.

True Love Waits was the slogan of a pro-chastity movement in America. And that was how Harper felt. She was open as to whether her husband would be a virgin, too. Most boys were desperate to do it and there were plenty of girls willing to accommodate them. So she wouldn't hold it against a man who'd had a lover, even a few lovers. That wouldn't stop him appreciating her saving herself for him. Was that fair? What if it wasn't? Life was unfair. Harper wasn't a feminist. She thought that men and women were equal, but different.

Jack wasn't giving up easily. 'Is the problem that you're scared of getting pregnant?'

'That comes into it, I suppose,' Harper said. 'And I certainly don't want to catch anything.'

'We're both virgins,' Jack reminded her. 'That's not an issue. Anyway, we'd use a condom, wouldn't we?'

Harper wouldn't let herself be trapped. 'We won't use a condom, no, because we won't be doing it.'

'But why? These days, most people don't marry until they're in their late twenties. Nobody's expected to be a virgin any more. It's too long to wait.'

'You're saying you want me to be average,' Harper said, sharply.

'No. You're twisting my words. I meant . . .'

She squeezed his hand. 'I *know* what you meant. You meant that I'm not gonna wait twelve or more years to have sex. I'm going to do it with someone sooner or later, so why on earth shouldn't I do it with you?'

'Yes,' Jack said. 'That's exactly what I meant.'

'Then I have to tell you you're wrong. When I get engaged, whether it's in two years or twelve years, I'm going to be a virgin. I'm saving myself. And it's not so unusual. There are lots of girls like me. You're going to have to get used to it.'

'I guess I am,' Jack said, ruefully.

Harper gave him a cuddle. 'It doesn't mean we can't do other things.'

Jack took a deep breath. A new negotiation was about to begin.

She wouldn't return his calls. One time, Iain got so desperate he tried the land line number, only to get her snotty godfather. *She doesn't want to talk to you*. Iain worried that he was losing his touch. First Zoe turned him down, then Meg kept him dangling for the best part of a month before running scared. Worse, Taz knew that Meg had dumped him. She now expected to be promoted from occasional screw to steady girlfriend, which was never on the cards. But he had to play her carefully, because they were at college together and she could create a stink.

Iain was tempted to ask out Meg's friend Nina. He'd had his eye on her since Year Nine, but she'd never been single before. He'd seen her in town the other day. She was with her mother, who was a bit tasty too. When he'd said hi, however, Nina had looked the other way.

Nina might not be interested, but he reckoned someone else was. Since Jan found out where he hid it, Iain had stopped keeping a diary. It was a childish thing to do anyhow, listing his conquests and the girls he planned to conquer.

If he were still keeping the diary, however, his recent entries would all have been about one person. Since seeing her at Meg's sixteenth, he'd been planning a campaign. This girl put Taz, Nina and Meg in the shade. Why she was wasting herself on a Joe Average like Jack Green was beyond Iain's comprehension. It was time for him to make exploratory moves.

In History, he manoeuvred himself to sit next to her. He hadn't fancied a girl so much since pursuing Zoe Cumberland. Over the last couple of weeks, he'd caught her glancing his way a couple of times. Studiously, he'd ignored her. This was a technique that usually worked for him. The more you ignored them, the more interested they got. Now he tossed her a few crumbs of conversation.

If Harper Simm knew Iain's reputation, she didn't let it show. She treated him like a regular guy. Turned out their dads worked together, so she'd get an invite to the company Christmas party at his house. Promising. As far as Harper knew, Iain was still going out with Meg. He did nothing to correct this impression. It was easier, with her thinking he was spoken for, to get her to talk about Jack.

'You two are mates, aren't you?' Harper asked at the end of a lesson.

'He seems to spend most of his time with you these days,' Iain replied.

'That's not true. A couple of evenings a week. I was thinking that the four of us ought to do something together. Go clubbing, or something.'

'Have you ever *been* to *Groucho*'s in Middleton? It's full of badly-dressed twenty- and thirty-somethings and the music's about twenty years out of date.'

'I don't think Jack would stand for that. He really keeps up with his music.'

'I don't know if he'd like to double date with Meg, either. They had a thing, not so long back.'

'For about five minutes, according to Jack,' Harper said. 'I'm sure it isn't a problem for him. Is it a problem for you? Is that why you two don't hang out?'

'No, not at all.' Since Iain turned fourteen, mates always took second place to mating, but he wasn't going to tell Harper this. 'So you and Jack are solid?'

Harper hesitated. Iain counted the beats. One meant nothing. Two was statistically negligible. Three was promising. Four preceded a lie. Harper took two and a half. 'We're fine. I mean, it's not like we're getting engaged, or anything.'

That was an odd thing to say, Iain thought. He upgraded Harper from *spoken for* to *promising*.

20

On Thursday night, Joe went out to 'meet someone for a drink'. Meg assumed this was the date he'd mentioned, but was too tactful to ask. If there was anything to tell, Joe would let her know when he was ready. Meg got on with her homework, then went round to see Bethany. Since her break-up with Ross, Beth had kept herself to herself even more than usual. Tonight, though, she wanted to go out.

'Where?' Meg asked.

'Anywhere we'll meet someone.'

'In Middleton, on a weekday night? You'll be lucky.'

Beth's mum drove them into town. She seemed relieved that Bethany was going out at all. The two girls went for a burger. The place was nearly empty.

'Why so down?' Meg wanted to know.

'I'm never going to have a boyfriend. Ever.'

'It's only a few months since your thing with Ross.'

'Ross doesn't count. It's hopeless. Look around us at school. There're a handful of people like you and Zoe who have boys after them all the time. You can choose who you go out with and how far you go with them.'

It hardly felt like that to Meg, but she didn't interrupt.

'Then there are a few like Nina, who might not be beautiful but are so confident that they can get pretty much what they want, simply by asking for it. Then there's the rest of us, who have to wait an age for real life to start, hoping and dreaming and snatching anything that comes along, even if it's really unsuitable.'

'Beth, what are you talking about? Firstly, look at Zoe and me. Neither of us have got boyfriends at the moment. Nor has Nina.'

'She could have Tom back tomorrow if she wanted. She's just hanging him out to dry until he agrees that he'll wait for her if she decides to go to uni.'

'I'm not sure about that. Maybe she's outgrown Tom. Anyhow, remember how you got off with Ross. If that could happen once—'

Beth interrupted with a bombshell. 'Ross turned out to be *thirteen years old*. He's in Year Nine.'

This took Meg completely by surprise. 'He lied about his age?'

'Not exactly. We both assumed . . .' Beth explained, at length. 'I expect it'll come out sooner or later. You're the first person I've told.'

'Not even Nina?'

'It's so humiliating.'

'You thought you were the same age when you were doing it. What's so humiliating about that? He didn't lie and neither did you. It was a misunderstanding. So what if he's two years younger than you? Tom's nearly four years older than Nina.'

'That's not all.' Beth blurted out that she and Ross hadn't even done it properly. He'd finished, it seemed, before he was inside her. Meg didn't know what to say. It was embarrassing, but not terribly surprising. There had always been something unreal about Beth's losing-her-virginity story.

'It doesn't matter,' she insisted to her friend. 'It's not a big deal.'

'Oh yes it is,' Beth said. 'And now I feel bad about having told you. I really ought to have told Nina first.'

'Then let's go round there now,' Meg suggested.

Nina's estate was on the edge of town, less than ten minutes' walk away. The girls decided against ringing first. Nina had packed in Tom and she'd packed in her job, too, wanting to concentrate on exams. Where else would she be but home?

Nina was Beth's best mate, Megan realised as they walked. Best to let them talk alone. But girls didn't walk round this part of Middleton on their own. Beth's dad would collect them both from Nina's. Meg had no choice but to tag along.

Nina's flat was on the third floor. Beth was about to ring the doorbell when they heard a loud, familiar laugh. Meg stood stock-still on the walkway.

'Is that who I think it is?' Beth asked.

Meg nodded. 'Maybe he's not with Nina. Maybe . . .'

But the next voice they heard was Nina's. 'You're so funny. You crack me up. Tell us another one.'

Beth and Meg looked at each other. 'Let's go back into town,' Beth said.

'He told me he had a date tonight,' Meg told Beth. 'I never imagined . . .'

'I saw them together,' Beth revealed, 'the night of your party. Out in the garden.'

'They were only talking,' Meg said. 'Neen had just split up with Tom. Joe helped her through it, she said.'

'I didn't say anything at the time, but I thought I saw them kissing.'

'You're kidding!' Meg said, though she could tell that Beth was serious.

'No, it was dark. It could have been a hug, not a kiss. But now we've seen . . . Neen always *did* like older guys.'

'Tom's only four years older than her. Joe's *twenty-one* years older!'

'I can't see how that would make any difference to Nina. What about Joe?'

'I don't know,' Meg replied.

They trudged back into town.

'How well do you know Iain Foster?' Harper asked Jack on Friday.

'As well as most people, I guess,' Jack said. 'He was in my form from when he arrived at Middleton Comp, halfway through Year Nine. His parents are loaded and he goes out with a lot of different girls. Why do you ask?'

'I got talking to him at the party the other week. And he's in my History class. He's an interesting enigma. Wherever he goes, there are girls eyeing him up, but he never appears to notice.'

'He notices all right,' Jack said. 'He just likes to play it cool. That way, it's even easier for him to bend them round his little finger.'

They kissed, but Harper's heart wasn't in it. Harper fancied Jack, in a safe, boy-next-door kind of way. He would never press her, no matter how excited he got, and was appreciative when she gave him a helping hand. But he wanted more, and things were never going to go any further than they had already gone.

Jack was easy company. Now and then, though,

Harper found herself getting bored. She was coming to realise that she liked being wooed and pursued. Until she met the right guy, Harper figured she'd have one or two steady boyfriends a year. The rest of the time, she'd play the field, dating when she felt like it. A girl ought to know what it was like to be independent. Three to four months was about the right length for a relationship. Which meant that Jack was nearing his sell-by date.

For the last couple of weeks, she'd been checking out Iain Foster. He was rather charismatic, and definitely charming. He was into sex, of course, but wasn't the sort of guy who would slip you a pill or force himself on you. Going out with him would be interesting. If his previous record was anything to go by, Iain would be fed up with Meg soon. Should Harper happen to be single by the time that happened, what was to stop the two of them getting together?

How close *were* Iain and Jack? Would Jack have told Iain that she was still a virgin, and meant to stay that way? No matter. Harper suspected that Iain, like her, loved a challenge. But Harper already knew who would be the victor.

'Iain's dad works with my dad,' Harper said. 'Did you know that?'

'No.'

'His parents are having this Christmas party for the families of people who work in my dad's division. Do you want to come with me?'

'I'm not family,' Jack said. 'You don't have to go, do you?'

'No, but I think I ought to. I spend so much time with you, I haven't made many friends yet. Can't hurt to check it out.'

'I guess not,' Jack said, but didn't volunteer to come, which suited Harper fine. If she decided to go out with Iain, she wasn't going to do it in a deceitful way. She would finish with Jack first. She had forewarned her boyfriend of her interest in someone else. Now she had to let him down gently.

21

Nina kept herself to herself at school. When Meg asked directly whether she was seeing anyone, the reply was, 'I've not taken Tom back yet, if that's what you mean. He only rings every other day now. Says he's giving me some space.'

Meg decided it would be better to talk to Joe before she talked to Nina. Nina was sixteen. Legally, she was an adult. She certainly had more experience of relationships than Meg's godfather. But Joe was the grown-up.

Catching Joe alone wasn't easy. As December arrived, he was busting a gut on all sorts of deadlines. Many places he did work for closed completely over Christmas and New Year. They needed Joe's cartoons done well in advance.

Joe also had a sideline in caricatures – jokey sketches which he did from photographs. Companies paid him a good whack to sketch senior executives in silly postures as Christmas gifts. This year, Joe had taken on more than he could manage, particularly as he kept going out at night.

Meg finally caught up with him late on Friday evening. Joe was e-mailing a sketch which had to be delivered to a magazine in New York by the end of the working day (it was 5pm there).

'I haven't eaten yet,' she told him. 'I thought we might have a meal together for once.'

'Good idea. Why don't you order pizza?'

Fifty minutes and six slices later, they were sharing the remains of a bottle of red. Joe put on a Ryan Adams concert he'd downloaded from the internet.

'This was only recorded last week,' he told her, and Meg pretended to be impressed. She knew that Joe missed living near a big city where there were gigs and clubs and independent cinemas. That was one reason he got so bound up in the internet. If Joe hadn't followed her family here, he'd probably be living in London by now.

'Sorry I've been so busy lately,' Joe said. 'Work will calm down after next week. It's always like this before Christmas.'

'What about your social life?' Meg asked. 'Will that calm down, too?'

'Sorry,' Joe said. 'I'm being a bit secretive, aren't I?'

Meg tried to be tactful. 'I know you're not used to sharing, but . . .'

'Truth is,' Joe said, 'I'm scared. Something's happening really fast and I'm out of my depth.'

Meg asked what he meant.

'Since Chris died,' Joe told her, 'there hasn't been anyone. I've tried enough times. Dinners, drinks, the odd gig or movies . . . I'd hesitate to call most of them dates. Nothing much ever came of them. Maybe things would have gone further sometimes if I'd asked . . . Then there's my career, which doesn't exactly enable me to meet women. What do I have to talk to women about? Alternative comics – that really gets 'em going, doesn't it? The only women I meet are on the internet. I guess I'm a classic nerd.'

'You're not a nerd,' Meg tried to assure him. 'You like cool stuff.'

'Rock music, you mean? But there are no decent gigs to take women to round here. And I can't dance, even if there were a good place to do that. I'm not like that Iain guy you dumped. I can't put pressure on women. I don't know how to chat them up. Thing is, I want a relationship, not casual sex. There'd be nothing casual about it for me. Because, before I could, you know, with someone, I'd need to be in love, like I was with Chris. And now, God help me, I think I'm falling and I'm terrified because she'll expect, and I've never . . .'

Meg was completely taken aback. She had no idea

what to say. It hadn't occurred to her that Joe might be as innocent as her. She could hardly warn him off Nina now, not when he had opened himself up so completely. 'Well, then,' she said, automatically quoting the teen magazines she used to scour for any trace of wisdom, 'if it's love, it'll work itself out. You don't have to get things perfect first time. If it feels right, go for it.'

The phone rang and Joe answered it. 'Great,' he said. 'Tomorrow night. I'll be there.' Putting down the phone, he told Meg, 'You're right. I'm going to go for it. That means I'm out again tomorrow night. Have you got plans?'

'I'm going to a party with Zoe,' Meg said. 'Some friend of a friend. They're short of girls, so Zoe's dragging the gang along.'

Except Nina, she remembered. Nina had excused herself, mumbling something about being away.

'Hope it's fun,' Joe said. 'I better get back to work. Thanks for discussing it with me. Funny thing for a father to be telling his daughter, huh?'

'If you put it in a book people wouldn't believe it,' Meg said.

When Joe was gone she dialled 1471 to check the number that had just called. It was Nina's.

* * *

190

Jack kept replaying that last conversation with Harper in his head. Why had she asked about Iain and the way so many girls fancied him? What was the comment she'd made? 'He never appears to notice.' *Probably because he's had half of them already*, Jack had thought, but not said. He wasn't sure how to tell Harper what Iain was like. If he went on about Iain's scorecard it would sound like he was criticising Harper's refusal to sleep with him. Yet he respected his girlfriend's position. No, respected was too strong a word. Understood. Something Iain could never do.

Was Iain still going out with Meg? Jack hadn't seen him for a while, but he'd probably have dumped her by now. Which meant he'd be looking for fresh meat. Maybe Jack *ought* to go to the company party with Harper. Middleton Chemicals was the biggest employer in town, so it was hardly a surprise that Harper's dad worked for Iain's. Jack had never been to Iain's house, but it was in the same, well-to-do part of town as Harper's. Jack remembered Iain's crude comment about her at Meg's party. Better to spend an evening being bored than leave Harper at the mercy of Iain Foster. Iain might still be going out with Meg but faithfulness was not high on his list of virtues.

On Saturday afternoon, Jack cycled over to Harper's. She'd been a little offhand with him all week, but his going to the party should fix the situation. It didn't matter that he wasn't invited. Iain was supposed to be a mate and it was his house.

Mr Simm let him in. 'She's in her room.' He called up to check that his daughter was 'decent', then sent Jack up. Harper was drying her hair, wearing only knickers and a bra. When he came in, she covered herself with a dressing gown, which was odd. She wasn't usually so coy.

'I'm glad you came.' Her tone was strange. 'I was going to call you.'

'What's up?'

Harper was brutal. 'There's no easy way to say this, Jack. It's been nice, but we've got as far as we're ever going to go. I think it's time we called it a day.'

'How can you know a thing like that?' Jack asked, taken by surprise. Every girl he'd been out with had dumped him. What had he done to deserve this?

'If we keep going over Christmas we're going to feel like an established couple. But we're too young to be serious and it worries me that you want more from this relationship than I do. I'm sorry.'

Jack knew there had to be more to this than she was saying. 'You're not doing this because you want to go out with Iain Foster, are you?'

'How can you say a thing like that?' Harper

protested, without conviction. 'I hardly know him.'

'I know Iain and how he impresses people. But you don't know what he's really like. He's a cheat and a user who's only interested in one thing.'

Somehow Harper managed to turn this around. 'He's supposed to be your friend and you talk about him like that!'

Jack pleaded with her. 'Don't tell me you're chucking me for Iain.'

'It's not like that,' Harper sounded anguished, but her eyes were dry. How long had she been working up to this? Jack left the room without saying goodbye.

He cycled round Middleton in the cold, thinking about revenge. Not against Harper, as such. She had a right to chuck him. It was true, to a point, that their relationship had run its course. There weren't all that many things they liked to do together. The thing he most wanted to do was denied him. Lately, their evenings often ended on a slightly sour note. But she wouldn't have chucked him if Iain hadn't been pursuing her. Jack guessed that Iain had been chatting her up in History lessons. He wished he'd told Harper exactly what Iain was like much earlier on. Anything he'd said today she was bound to take as sour grapes.

'Jack!' He recognised the voice calling his name, but, for a moment, couldn't place the girl with the glasses and the short hair. 'What are you doing round here?'

'Just riding my bike, the way us little boys do,' Jack told Zoe Cumberland, newly transfigured into a kooky character from an alternative comic. 'How about you?'

'Picking up a bottle to take to a party tonight. You look cold. Want to come in for a coffee?'

'I'd love to,' Jack said.

'I thought maybe you'd been to see Harper,' Zoe said, showing him where to put his bike.

'I have. For the last time.'

'Don't tell me you finished with her?' Jack was about to explain when Zoe added, 'I thought better of you than that.'

'How do you mean?' Jack asked, not clear what his offence was.

'I had a long chat with Harper at Meg's sixteenth. She was telling me about how she was going to stay – you know – until she was engaged. She also said that her last boyfriend dumped her because she wouldn't change her mind. I told her you weren't like that.'

'Thanks,' Jack said.

'But I was wrong.'

'No. You were right about me, wrong about her. She's dumped me so that she can go out with Iain Foster.'

'You're kidding!'

Jack shook his head. Zoe sat down. 'Boy,' she said. 'One of them is in for a shock.'

Jack tried to laugh but failed.

'There's this party tonight,' Zoe said. 'Nothing special. A friend of a guy I once went out with, boarding school boys who are short of girls. A bunch of us are going. You look like you need some company. If you brought a couple of your mix tapes, then at least we'd know there'd be good dance music. Want to come?'

Meg had spent all of Saturday trying to get into a conversation with Joe and failing. He was shopping for their trip to Australia, buying clothes for his date that night and having yet another haircut. He had more colour in his cheeks than Meg could remember since the time he joined them on holiday in the Lake District.

She didn't know what to do. She couldn't discuss the Joe and Nina situation with either of her parents. Australia was ten hours ahead. They would already be asleep. Perhaps the best thing to do was to talk it over with Nina.

'Sorry, she isn't here,' Pauline, Nina's mum said.

'Do you know when she'll be back?'

'You know Nina. She's a law unto herself these days. I'll tell her you called, but I'm going out tonight, so I may miss her.'

An hour later, Joe emerged, ready for his evening. He was wearing a black shirt with grey jeans and Italian shoes.

'You look tremendous,' he told her, admiring her party outfit.

'Thanks.' Meg was going to have one last go at bringing up the subject of Nina, but, just then, the taxi they were sharing to the other side of town turned up. She couldn't talk about Nina with a stranger in front, and Joe seemed nervous, too, so the journey took place in silence. Meg wondered whether she should tell the others tonight. She had to tell someone. But she couldn't tell them the whole story, how her father was a virgin and, if anything, Nina was the one making all the running. It was too sad. And what if she'd got something wrong?

When the taxi let her out at the party, Meg heard Joe telling the taxi driver the next address to go to. Nina's address. It was too late to do anything about it now.

22

The party started early in the evening. Iain had to be on his best behaviour. No getting drunk for him, though the other guests were encouraged to drink their fill. All of Dad's section was here, partner and kids in tow, along with a couple of Dad's bosses and their families. Last year's do had been deadly. Iain had escaped early to be with his girlfriend. This year, there was no-one to escape to.

Iain did his best to charm everyone he met. Soon he found himself playing snooker against the son of the Divisional Director, being careful not to win by too many points. His dad came by, showing round some guests Iain didn't recognise. They had a son the age of his opponent and Iain ceded the snooker table to him. The small, slightly severe-looking father beamed his appreciation.

'I believe you know our daughter,' he said. 'Harper.'

'Of course. We're in the same History group. Has she not come tonight?'

'She's talking to your sister in the kitchen,' Dad said.

'Oh, right. I'll go and say hello then.' Iain cleared out quickly. He didn't want Janine saying anything which might put Harper off him.

Jan was wearing a backless dress which was too old for her. It reminded Iain of a swimming costume. Spotting him, Harper raised her glass of fizzy wine.

'I see you already know my brother,' Janine said.

'Doesn't everyone?' Harper replied, brightly.

'Everyone who looks like you,' Jan said, before sloping away.

'No Jack?' Iain asked Harper. 'I thought he might . . .'

'I didn't think he was invited,' Harper said, then lowered her voice. 'Which turned out to be for the best. We split up this afternoon.'

'I'm sorry. I didn't see that coming.' Iain kept a very straight face.

'He was getting too serious,' Harper said. 'I just want to have fun.'

'I know exactly what you mean,' Iain said. 'Meg was starting to get a bit clingy and . . .'

'You and Meg have finished too?'

'A couple of weeks ago,' Iain told her.

'I'm sorry.'

'Don't be,' Iain said, with an expansive shrug. 'I'm not.'

'OK. I guess life's too short to be tied down.'

'You're not into bondage?' Iain teased and Harper laughed. This was going brilliantly. He hadn't expected her to flirt with him so easily.

'Two weeks . . .' Harper said. 'I'm surprised you haven't found a replacement yet.'

'It's true I've got something of a reputation as a ladies' man,' he said.

'It hadn't escaped my notice.' Harper gave him a coy smile.

'But if somebody starts getting really serious, I run a mile. We don't have to wish our whole lives away before we've even left home.'

'I couldn't agree more,' Harper said. 'And there are some things in life which mean more the longer you have to wait for them.'

Iain wasn't sure what she meant by this last comment, but he nodded appreciatively. 'I'd really like to get to know you better,' he said.

'You're in luck,' Harper told him. 'We've got all evening.'

Leah was used to feeling like a spare part at parties. She saw herself as the unlovely friend who only gets lucky at the end of the night, if at all. Tonight, at least, the rest of her friends were in the same boat: single. Or so she thought. Zoe's dad was taking them. Zoe, having changed her image and sworn off boys, nevertheless had Jack Green beside her in the car. Wasn't he going out with Harper? Best not to ask.

'Who else is coming?' she asked Zoe.

'Meg. Nina's busy. Parvinder's visiting Sanjeev at university. Beth said she might make it later on, if she felt like it.'

Zoe's dad dropped them off. The party was crowded. Most people there were sixth formers. They were friends of a friend of Zoe's who hadn't gone to Middleton Comp. It was a good feeling, being among people who didn't remember what you looked like as a stick insect, aged eleven. But most of the lads at the party were rugby players – hardly Leah's type. Come to think of it, she still had no idea what her type was. Until she found out, Leah was willing to experiment.

After a couple of drinks, she began to relax. She leant against Zoe, who was drinking more than normal. Maybe she was going to be less of a control freak now that she had a new image. Leah found it easier to talk to this Zoe. They shared a giggly conversation.

'I really like your new look,' Leah said. 'It's brainy but not intimidating.'

'I'll take that as a compliment,' Zoe said. 'You look fantastic tonight, by the way. That top is killer.'

Something made Leah a little uncomfortable. 'Better go and see what I can hunt down with it,' she told her friend, tossing her hair back. 'Wish me luck.'

Zoe smiled enigmatically, but said nothing.

By ten, the party at the Fosters had separated into clusters. All the families with young children had gone home. So, to Iain's relief, had Harper's parents. They were too up themselves for comfort. Iain could hardly make a move on Harper if her mum or dad was liable to walk by at any moment. That only left her brother to worry about. He was in the games room on the PS2. According to Harper, he would happily remain there for hours.

Where to take her? His room was unavailable, as it was being used for guests' coats. This was probably a deliberate ploy on Iain's parents' part.

He got Harper another drink. As he left, a drunken sales executive told her how beautiful she was and wondered who was lucky enough to be her husband.

'Actually,' Harper said, 'I'm single. And I think your boss is my dad.'

The guy hurried off. Iain admired that kind of feistiness. This was a girl he could go out with for ages, a girl he wouldn't mind being faithful to.

'Where have you been all my life?' he asked her.

'Avoiding guys who use cheesy lines like that,' she said. 'Can we go somewhere quieter?'

'Sure. My room's full of coats, but we could try—'

'Let's stay downstairs,' Harper interrupted. 'We don't want people to start talking.'

'Good point,' Iain said.

As they entered the empty dining room, Harper tripped. She was a little tipsy, something Iain was usually able to turn to his advantage. He caught her, clasping her arm, gently pulling her towards him. Their first kiss lasted a long time.

'You're a good kisser,' she said.

'So are you,' he told her, pushing the door to the room firmly shut. They kissed again. 'Will you go out with me?' he asked her.

She nibbled his ear. 'I heard you specialised in one night stands.'

'Not with you,' he promised.

Her breasts swelled against his chest. They kissed hungrily, pressed up against the snooker table, feeling each other up like their lives depended on it. But when his hands reached inside her dress, she pulled away.

'Too much,' she said.

'I want you,' he told her. 'I seriously want you. Please go out with me.'

'I only split up with Jack today,' she told him, breathily. 'Ask me again next week and I might go out with you. Though I have to warn you: I set limits.'

'I'll do anything you say,' Iain informed her, earnestly. 'Anything at all.'

Meg was glad when the others arrived. It was no fun, being at a party where you didn't know anybody. A couple of guys had tried to chat her up, but they'd both been too full of themselves, too Iain-like. Meg spotted Zoe first, surprised to find that she'd made no concessions to being at a party.

'Still dressing down, I see,' Meg said. 'How's that working for you?'

'Outstandingly,' Zoe told Meg. 'I feel more anonymous, in control.'

'Getting less attention doesn't mean that you're in control,' Meg said.

'It means I can talk to you without being hassled,' Zoe pointed out.

As if to prove the point, a guy tapped Meg on the shoulder. 'Can I get you a drink?'

Meg held up her half full glass of cider.

'Oh, right. Want to dance?'

'Maybe later, if the music gets better. I'm talking now.'

As Meg turned back to Zoe, she spotted someone. 'What's Jack doing here?'

'He came with me.'

This really threw Meg. 'You and Jack? A couple?'

'That's not what's happening,' Zoe said. 'I ran into Jack earlier. Harper dumped him today.'

'No!' Meg remembered herself and tried to act just a little dismayed. 'They seemed such a great couple at my party.'

'It gets worse. Jack reckons she dumped him so that she could go out with, wait for it, *Iain Foster*.'

'She's welcome to him,' Meg said. Then, because it was Zoe, and they trusted each other, she asked what was really on her mind. 'So, tell me, *are* you interested in Jack?'

Zoe shook her head and gave Meg a frank gaze. 'The question is, are *you*?'

'I had my chance. I didn't treat him well. So I ought to wish you luck.'

'But you wouldn't say no to a second chance,' Zoe guessed.

Meg didn't argue.

'You know, the first thing he asked me when I told him about this party was, *Is Meg going*?'

While Meg thought about this, Zoe breezed off and joined Leah, who was standing on her own, gently swaying to the music, ignoring a guy who was trying to attract her attention. Someone coughed. Meg turned and Jack was right beside her.

'It's good to see you,' she said. 'Zoe just told me. I'm—'

'I'll live,' he cut her off.

'Did you bring one of your mix tapes?' she asked him.

'Sure. Zoe asked me to.'

'Now might be a good time to put it on.'

Jack took the tape over to Zoe who, with her usual tact, negotiated replacing the bland music which was playing. While she was doing this, Beth arrived. As Jack's tape began, people poured on to the dance floor. Meg was about to dance herself when, promisingly, Jack rejoined her. They were alone in a corner.

'I am sorry about Harper, though,' Meg said. 'You two seemed good together.'

'I thought so,' Jack said. 'But cracks were beginning to show. Harper's got this really fun, flirtatious side. She comes on strong. But she's from this uptight, religious family, which kind of comes out in some of the things she does and says.'

'You seemed to have a lot in common.'

'Not really. We liked some of the same books and

films, but completely different music. And we're from very different backgrounds.'

'You liked each other. Shouldn't that be enough?' Meg asked.

Jack paused to think about it. 'She's the first girl I've been out with for more than about five minutes, so I've nothing to compare her with. You tell me.'

'I've got even less experience of a long-term thing.' Meg paused, choosing her words carefully. 'I'm sorry I knocked you back earlier this year.'

'You had every right to.'

'No, I hadn't. You didn't do anything wrong. It was pretty dumb of me.'

'Forget it,' Jack told her. 'It did me good to work up the nerve to ask you out. At least you said "yes". If you'd turned me down flat I'd never have had the nerve to chat up Harper.'

'Maybe you'll have better luck with Zoe,' Meg told him.

Jack laughed. 'Me and Zoe? I don't think so.'

Meg was relieved to hear this, but couldn't resist asking. 'Why?'

'I don't think of her that way at all.'

'It's weird she's not your type.'

'I don't have a type,' Jack told her, then swallowed his next sentence. 'Maybe if she was more like you . . .'

'Pardon?' Meg said.

'You heard me,' Jack said.

Meg was silenced. The music swelled. Jack grinned nervously, then raised his voice. 'Did you notice I stopped smoking?'

'Yes,' she shouted. 'I noticed. Why did you do that?'

'It was the only reason I could think of for you dumping me.'

'Not much of a reason,' Meg admitted.

'And now it's gone.'

He took his chance, leaning forward to kiss her. Meg kissed him right back.

Harper looked at her watch. 'How long have we been in here? I need to get home. Where the hell's my brother?'

'He probably left already,' Iain said. 'Everybody else has.'

'Call me a taxi while I check if his coat's gone.'

'No need for a taxi. My dad's hired a driver and a car for the evening to take everyone back. He doesn't like to risk any drink-driving incidents.'

'OK,' Harper said, 'I'll look for Ross. Could you get my coat?'

She described both her coat and her brother's. Iain went up to his room to get them, feeling on top of the world. He was smitten by Harper Simm, completely smitten. Tonight, she'd made him go easy, making it clear she wasn't going to rush into bed with him. That was OK. Some things were worth waiting for. Anyhow, she couldn't be a tougher nut to crack than Meg.

He picked up Harper's coat. Her brother's was still there, too. Where could Ross be? The last time Iain had seen him he was playing some video game with Jan. Possibly they were watching something in her room. Iain decided to check.

Harper had only dumped Jack earlier today, that was another reason for her not to rush things. Tough on Jack. First Meg knocked him back, then Iain stole Harper from under his nose. And she hadn't even given him any. That much, Harper had made abundantly clear. She'd also made it clear that Jack suspected Iain of pursuing her. When Jack found out that Iain had won, they'd no longer be mates. Tough.

Jan's room was at the back of the house, beside the second bathroom. He knocked on the door. No answer. Iain tried the door anyway. It was locked.

'Jan, are you in there? I'm looking for Harper's brother.'

'Just a minute.' What was she *doing* in there? Iain had a fleeting suspicion, but dismissed it. Jan was barely thirteen, too young to be anybody's girlfriend. And Ross was a young Christian goody-goody. Jan couldn't be in safer hands.

'Sorry,' his sister said, opening the door. 'Didn't realise it was locked. Habit. Ross wanted to see the new Eminem video.'

'Whatever,' Iain said, glancing at Ross, who seemed embarrassed to be found in a girl's room. 'Ross, your sister's ready to go. There's a car waiting.'

Iain hurried back down to Harper, enjoying the thrill of anticipation, the engimatic promise etched across her face. He couldn't wait to make love to her.

23

'How are you going to explain this to your parents?'
Meg asked Jack. They'd been up all night, talking
mostly. After watching dawn break, they'd got into her
bed, but neither had slept. Now they were upstairs,
where Meg was preparing some breakfast.

'I'll think of something. How are you going to
explain it to Joe? Want me to sneak out?'

'No need.' She handed him a mug of coffee. 'I
checked his room. He didn't come home last night.'

Jack made a phone call, then returned. 'It's all right.
They assumed I'd been at this party I'd mentioned and
stayed the night at Iain's.'

'That's good,' Meg said. 'I wouldn't want to get you
into trouble.'

She kissed him passionately. Fooling around with
Jack was entirely different from making out with Iain.
It felt like they were starting out on something, taking
the thing at their own speed. It was special. Meg was
about to suggest they share a bath when they both

heard the front door open. Quickly, they pulled apart.

'A visitor!' Joe said, walking into the living room with a big smile on his face. 'Nice to see you again, Jack.'

'And you,' Jack said. 'Hey, did you see the new issue of *Optic Nerve*'s out? First one in two years.'

'Good things are worth waiting for,' Joe said, with a boyish smirk. 'You know, Adrian Tomine's stuff reminds me of . . .'

And, just like that, they were off. Meg sighed exasperatedly. After a couple of minutes, she managed to interrupt.

'How was your night, Joe? No problems?'

'None at all.' Joe's smile told her all she needed to know. Meg wanted to ask about Nina. But she couldn't do that in front of Jack.

'In fact,' Joe went on, 'when we go to Sydney at Christmas, we might not be on our own. I don't think Pat and Sarah will mind if I bring a friend, do you?'

'*Nina?*' Meg blurted out, wondering how on earth Pat and Sarah would react.

'Oh, she'll be fine. Nina and Tom are back together. He's got this little flat and I expect she'll want to spend Christmas here with him.'

'*Nina and Tom.*' Meg needed to check what she'd just heard. '*Flat?*'

'Hasn't she told you?' Joe said. 'Tom's moved into a one-bedroom flat on the far side of town. Nina stayed last night, helping him sort the place out.'

'And you know this because . . . ?'

Joe smiled. 'Because of Pauline, of course. She's fine with it.'

Jack worked it out more quickly than Meg did. 'You're going out with Nina's mum, Pauline?'

'That's right,' Joe said. 'Do you know her?'

'Yeah. She's terrific, Pauline. You're a lucky bloke.'

'And so are you,' Joe said, playfully punching Jack in the chest. 'You'd better treat my daughter well.'

'*Daughter*?' Jack looked at Meg, confused.

She flopped on to a chair. 'This is too much to take in at once,' she said. 'I'll explain in a minute.'

Jack and Joe beamed at each other, happy men. Everything was all right, Meg realised. Everything was a lot better than all right. But this new situation might take a little time to get used to. Behind her, the phone began to ring.

'That'll be your parents,' Joe said to Meg. 'Will you talk to them first, or shall I?'

Parvinder and Zoe pretended to work on their project, but kept coming back to the party the night before.

'So Beth got off with a rugby player,' Parvinder said. 'Imagine.'

'She went to watch him play today. A new pastime for Sundays.'

'Rather her than me,' Parvinder said. 'Still, I'm glad Meg's with Jack. I've always thought they were suited. Did he really go home with her?'

'*I told you*. When I rang up earlier, she said he'd stayed the night. That can only mean one thing.'

'I guess,' Parvinder replied, hesitantly.

'It's just you and me now – the last virgins in the gang.'

'Actually . . .' Parvinder began, with an embarrassed smile.

Not much surprised Zoe, but this did. 'You and Sanjeev? This weekend?'

'The first time was the weekend of Meg's party,' Parvinder admitted. 'We got carried away and . . . suddenly it seemed silly not to. We had a house to ourselves, and we're getting married in a year or two. So, why not?'

'Was it . . . everything you wanted?'

'It gets better every time,' Parvinder said.

They talked about Sanjeev until it was almost time for Zoe's dad to collect her. Parvinder was relieved that she could finally share the story with someone. But it was a pity that Zoe had nothing to share. Her friend had never been out with anybody she really liked. Parvinder thought she knew why.

'What about you and Leah last night? Did either of you get lucky?'

'I had a couple of offers,' Zoe said.

'But they were the wrong kind of buyers,' Parvinder suggested carefully.

'Something like that.' Zoe sighed. 'Leah didn't get off with anybody either.'

Parvinder had long since guessed which way Zoe was inclined. None of the others seemed to have any idea – especially, unfortunately, Leah. When talking to Zoe, Parvinder was careful never to spell it out. She figured her friend was more comfortable that way. But now Parvinder risked a question.

'You really like Leah, don't you?'

'Is it that obvious?' Zoe asked, wistfully. 'I don't even know if she's . . .'

Her voice trailed off, as though she'd given too much away.

'I don't suppose she knows herself yet,' Parvinder suggested. 'When did you know?'

'About me? Iain Foster was my last attempt to convince myself I was straight. But I've always liked Leah that way. I just wouldn't admit it to myself.'

'Give it time. If you're right about her, she'll work it out. One of these days.'

Outside, a car sounded its horn. Zoe gathered up her papers, put them in a folder, then gave Parvinder a rare hug.

'One of these days,' she repeated ruefully, then said goodnight.

A few minutes later, Parvinder was ready to turn in. She said goodnight to her parents and returned to her room. On the wall, above the bed, was a photo of the six of them from two years ago: the gang. Only two years, but each girl seemed like a child to her now. Especially herself.

Parvinder took it down. She removed the photo from the frame and slid it carefully into her scrapbook. Then she replaced the photo with one that Sanjeev had given her earlier in the day, just before she boarded the bus for home. His face would be the last thing she saw before going to sleep every night. For ever, she prayed, and ever.

A note from the author

This one's for my agents,
Jenny and Penny Luithlen, with
thanks for their patient support,
particularly at those times when I can't keep
away from controversial areas. I'd also like to
thank: Anne Cassidy, for giving me back the title,
and Venetia Gosling, for letting me keep it; Eileen
Armstrong and the Cramlington Litcritters, for their
comments on the first draft (some of which made it
on to the back cover!); Zed, Barbara (you know
what for) and, as always, Sue. Don't you hate
writers who end their books with a list of
acknowledgements which reads like
an Oscar speech? Me too.